CW00433184

Dedicated to my mother and father

Beryl and Len

"The distinction between the past, present and future is only a stubbornly persistent illusion"

Albert Einstein (1879-1955)

"The history of science shows that theories are perishable. With every new truth that is revealed we get a better understanding of Nature and our conceptions and views are modified."

Nicola Tesla (1856-1943)

Introduction

Reality is socially constructed through our interaction with other people and through our own thinking. Different people interpret the physical world in different ways because we each have our own interpretation of an existence.

As the author, I am not trying to impose a vision on you as the reader, but helping you to release your own. Have you ever reflected on your own being?

When I started out writing this novel, there was a great need to understand what exactly was going on in our lives and how we integrated within the bigger picture. I questioned my own state of living and origins. I realised that I was in fact part of a storyline. The only aspect I wasn't sure about was how long this story had existed, and where it fitted into the grand scheme and design of our lives, our world and its overall actuality.

I began to study current trends and statistics that revealed a pattern throughout our short-lived history. I realised that there appeared a potential cycle in the way in which life, societies and civilisations evolved... effectively rediscovering itself. Could it be that we are one instance in this re-cycle of existence?

The trends were taken from our recent times and extrapolated into the future; they revealed a path which is told in the storyline you are about to read. It will demand questions you may wish to ask of yourself, and where you fit into this cycle of evolution. You yourself may start to doubt your own conscience and spirituality.

It is hoped that as you progress through the novel you will open your mind to what has been before us, and to that which could follow. You may even start to question your notions of what is the truth – physical, emotional, historical, scientific and artistic...

This tale will take you on an exciting and challenging journey that will hopefully help you to re-evaluate your own reality.

Leonard Page.

1. Old Friends

It is summer 2006 and a beautiful sun-scorched day in London. Hyde Park was playing host to thousands of visitors who were either strolling aimlessly through the picturesque gardens or resting to savour the joy, peace and serenity of their surroundings.

For teenager Richard Braxton, a hard-working, conscientious and ambitious 19-year-old university student, it was a perfect day to lie on the grass and study for his forthcoming exams. With his head full of facts and figures, he needed peace and quiet. No unwelcomed interruptions from his friends or family. A time to escape and a time to breathe, take it slow and soak up even more information from his books. He had picked an ideal place to study, just behind a large bush and in the shade. It allowed him to monitor the comings and goings in the park, while at the same time it gave him his privacy.

There is something comforting and rewarding about lying in the park, with the scent of freshly mowed grass under the cover of a hypnotic clear blue cyan sky. After an hour, Braxton had dozed off into a deep sleep. He was lying on a cosy soft blanket, and with the heat of the sun, together with the intense studying, had brought on an impromptu siesta.

When he finally awoke, he was quite surprised to have drifted off, but felt invigorated for it, feeling much more alert and ready for further studying.

In the background, on the other side of the bush, a wooden park bench was set back slightly away from the path. Two old men were sitting upright on the bench with their backs to Braxton. He hadn't noticed them before – perhaps they had arrived during his nap.

He became captivated by these two men, who occasionally would gaze about, soaking in the wonderful panorama of tranquillity. Braxton started to realise that these weren't just two regular old men, but two very tall men, who almost dwarfed their seats. Both were very gaunt, ancient in appearance and awkwardly unnatural to the eye.

Braxton was now totally distracted. He had completely forgotten about his studies as he was pulled into the men's conversation. They were whispering... yet perhaps they weren't, for they weren't cupping their hands around their mouths to whisper, but simply speaking very softly. Weird really, because most old men are renown for speaking loudly due to faltering hearing. Yet, whilst Braxton's hearing was impeccable, he couldn't help but creep closer to the men in order to listen intently into their discussion.

Perhaps it was their unusual appearance that made him feel drawn into their exchange. He wanted to know who they were and what they were chatting about.

His intrigue with their personas made him focus. They were both so very tall that they looked like two adults perched on a child's chair; with their feet resting far from the bench and their knees still higher than their waists. Bizarrely, they were both dressed in black – hardly the clothing for a hot summer's day! One was wearing a black hood, whilst the other wore a large black cowboy hat – perhaps to keep the sun from his eyes, in addition to his dark sunglasses. In contrast, their complexions were so pale – so blanched. At one point, when one of them turned to survey the grounds, Braxton managed to take a closer look. He was shocked at the man's gaunt appearance, with his face full of wrinkles. It almost gave them a reptilian appearance.

Braxton tuned into their discussion.

"You know, my friend, this has to be my favourite place, space and time," said the hooded man contentedly.

"On a summer's day, like today, I totally agree! I love it here. Although we shouldn't really expose ourselves to such radiation, you know," replied the cowboy man.

"This place is so special. It's quite surreal, to see these people passing by. They're completely blind to what's happening... even as we speak," continued the hooded man.

"Oh yes! They are so young that they all look like children... and in many ways they really are in the grand scheme of things, don't you think? It's amazing to see the changes in their humanity... in their societies. I still can't believe we have been privy to everything... such a privilege! I don't think they will ever comprehend the true scale of space and time, and how their little world fits into the universal state of everything. We must guard this phenomenon, as we have done for thousands of years," answered the cowboy.

Braxton was now confused. They talked of riddles... of other dimensions. He even heard them compare their ages, and it simply defied normality – ridiculous! They spoke of an impossible age – they had to be lying, it was the only explanation.

Braxton dared not breathe for fear of being detected.

They spoke of today as though they were watching a movie; measuring it for its place in history and how it compared to other times. They spoke about the past... but also of the future! Impossible! They said that we, the people of today, needed to understand how the world and the universe really works. There was a surface of society where everyone had their role, and followed it due to conditioning and programming. They said we needed to open our minds and consider what was happening to us over a greater span of millennia, not just about what had come before us but also what was to follow. The men said the past could be our future, and that our future could be in our past. Wow! What did they mean? And again they kept saying it. "One day, it will hit them when they least expect it! And what has come may have done so not just from our past, but also from our future. Their lateral thinking will develop until it is the norm again."

These were riddles, surely! Very confusing.

Braxton shifted his aching arm and accidentally caught a small twig on the ground with his elbow, and immediately the two men stood up to leave. Lying on the grass, Braxton stared up at these two giants of men as he would a skyscraper, for they were so very tall and gangly. He also noticed their hands were bony to match their gaunt features.

As they slowly strolled pass Braxton, they both peered down and nonchalantly said: "Good day to you, young man." Braxton could only mumble and look to the ground. He was embarrassed, knowing that these men had known all along that he had been eavesdropping on their meeting. If they did know, perhaps their conversation had been a hidden message for Braxton to relay.

Braxton's last thought was… as he gazed down at the grass… "Open your mind. Do not think of your past, or of your future, but consider they happen and are intertwined throughout our universe. Open your mind… try to understand!"

Braxton leapt to his feet and returned to the path… but both men had vanished.

2. Storm

Welcome to the early 21st Century. It's 2015, and recently there has been a number of predictions for the end of the world. These predictions have been either foretold by ancient civilisations or by modern day psychics. Some might say these psychics are just loonies or crackpot conspirators. All of them thriving on the fear factor, or profiting by selling books on this crazy theme and creating followers.

Most world leaders are collectively sending out warnings and adopting measures to safeguard our beautiful planet. Others think it is just one huge wicked conspiracy or a deliberate act to encourage scaremongering. Perhaps one day the world will find out, perhaps when it is all too late! It may not happen, maybe not in our lifetime, but sadly it will affect generations to come.

Recently the weather has become rather noticeably unstable. This includes last night's heavy storm. It was a storm of all storms, with thunder and lightning of a magnitude not seen for many years – a violent storm to remember. There has been a series of major storms across the world, including hurricanes in and around America and the Caribbean. There have even been severe storms and flooding in Europe. Britain is no exception, and last night's storm was long overdue.

Perhaps it was due to the global warming that everyone has been talking about. After all, the world's climate is changing, or so the so-called experts would have us believe.

It was a typical cold, damp November evening in the Nottinghamshire countryside. The days were short and the nights were long. More often than not it was raining, and when it rained, it was constant, pouring down relentlessly.

Outside, one could smell the smoke from the numerous chimneys in the towns and villages. It was a warm and inviting odour where wood or coal fires had been lit. It was the kind of evening when one would choose to stay indoors by the fire. An ideal time for a bowl of hot soup or a pot of steaming stew to warm the body and soul. So when the storm started at around 10pm, most people were already settled in their cosy homes for the evening.

The storm was more fascinating than the TV or a blockbuster movie. Most people watched out of their windows, gazing at the flashes of lightning. It was a light show worthy of a commemorative firework display, similar to Bonfire Night or Bastille Day all over again. Perhaps we should be celebrating this force of Mother Nature in all its magnitude and majesty.

The storm carried its own rhythm, and it would have been fitting to accompany the whole show with Wagner's Ride of the Valkyries, as cymbals crashed to the flashes of lightning. It would have been an appropriate synchronisation to this mesmerising performance.

Needless to say the majority of people and animals didn't sleep well during this violent performance.

When dawn ultimately broke the next morning, the storm had long since passed, calm and serenity had been restored in the area as everyone greeted the new day. The sky was clear with not a single cloud. There was no wind, the air was clear, and the sun started caressing the houses and landscape – it was going to be a beautiful day. One could almost hear the subtle sounds of Edvard Grieg's Peer Gynt Suite No. 1 in the background.

Isn't it incredible how Mother Nature can be so cruel and hurtful in one evening, damaging so much beauty and life? Yet the next day, she lays a soothing ointment on the wounds she has inflicted.

3. Cemetery

Mike Stevens arrived early as usual for his daily shift at the St. Wilfrid cemetery, in Nottingham. He was always the one to open the large heavy black wrought iron gates. They were cold to the touch as he swung them open and locked them in to place. He drove carefully through the winding narrow gravel path ascending to the main building and parked his car in his usual spot to the rear, where the workers had an entry into their office. There was something very satisfying in being the first person on site in the mornings, giving him a warm feeling of contentment.

Mike was in his mid-30s with short dark hair and a small bald patch starting at the back of his head. One could often see him wearing a cap or hat, especially in the extreme cold of winter or the high temperatures of a sunburnt summer. He had worked hard as a groundsman after leaving school, then moved into park management, and was now managing the grounds at the local cemetery – a position he enjoyed greatly.

Mike preferred to be hands-on. So whilst his primary role was managing the grounds and burials, he was also not averse to having his hands dirty. He loved gardening and delving deep in the soil and dirt, breathing in the earthy fragrance of the land, the freshly cut grass, appreciating the range of colours and perfumes of spring and summer flowers, and the diversity of the four seasons.

He lived with his wife and two young children, and spent most of his spare time on the allotment he owned. It was approximately a 25-minute drive from the cemetery, on the other side of town. He tried to be as organic as possible and prided himself on the crops he would reap and bring home to the family at the weekends.

Mike was a strong, methodical and well-organised individual, a very approachable and down to earth person, very much wearing his heart on his sleeve. Above all he was a family and team man. To him, he would go so far as to say that his team at work was an extension of his family.

As always, when Mike opened and entered the office, he could smell the age of the building, with its odour of musk – although some would call it damp. But Mike knew that during the course of the day there would be other familiar odours that all formed part of their working environment. Instinctively, Mike's first duty every morning was to go immediately to the kettle and teapot, without fail, for his welcomed morning infusion of a good old cup of English Breakfast tea. Instantly, the delicate sweetness of tea would perfume the air, and the smell of musk would gradually disappear. He would also switch on and listen to the radio to bring some life and sound into the office. Typically it was tuned in to the local station, who would play a good mixture of popular music as well as the local news and weather.

Mike was always first in to work. He wasn't a great sleeper and since his childhood he had always been the first to rise, first to breakfast and first to his cup of tea. It was those first few cups that woke him up and gave him his fuel for the day.

Joyce Smith and Colin Devlin were Mike's colleagues. They would arrive every morning knowing that Mike would have their hot tea ready on their desks. More often than not, Joyce would bring along some home-made cake that she had baked the previous evening. Mike was never quite sure whether the cake Joyce brought into the office was surplus from the night before, or if she had made extra batches especially for the team. The smell of freshly baked cakes augmented the office's odour of sweet fragrant tea. The morning tea and cake routine was the best way to start their day, especially on cold and wet winter days.

Joyce was a buxom curly redhead with dark auburn hair, matching round rosy cheeks and hands that carried a lavender fragrance of a moisturising hand cream that she often applied throughout the day. She was approaching her 50s and adored her work. She was married with three older children, one of whom had already started working in a nearby town at a plant nursery, while the other two were still at a local college. Joyce was very much an adoring mother and considered both Mike and Colin as her adopted sons. In fact she often said she had five children to care for in her family. Her husband worked locally for social services. He was a large man in many ways, as he was fed by a woman who loved to cook almost every evening.

In contrast, Colin was a skinny 22-year-old with long chestnut hair, whose appearance implied he was a peace-loving hippie. He didn't give out too much detail about his life, as he was a quiet and modest lad generally, but both Mike and Joyce were reliably informed that he was dating at the moment. He had left school with few qualifications, but had a heart of gold and a good work ethic. These were qualities recognised by Mike immediately when he had interviewed Colin three years before, and he had never regretted recruiting him since. Colin's humour was quite dry and subtle, often relating to his job. His typical joke would follow the question: "Do you dig graves?" Whereupon, his response would be "Yeah! They're pretty cool, man!" with two fingers in the air, signalling peace and love… hippie man.

Mike was very happy and content with his team colleagues.

With cake and tea in their hands the threesome were discussing the previous night's storm – the intensity, the luminosity, the volume and frequency. It had ended at perhaps about 4am. And as often with these storms, the regularity of the sights and sounds had finally put them to sleep.

The radio had reported a number of deaths caused by the malevolent storm. Lightning had viciously struck. Trees had fallen. It made one realise how fragile the world was.

Earlier that morning, when Mike had driven his aging car up the cemetery path, he noticed a new grave that had been dug close to the rear entrance of the main building. He had not been in work the day before, so he asked his colleagues about the number of graves that had been dug on that day. Both Joyce and Colin were a little confused, quite certain that no new graves had been made. The two of them looked at each other in an inquisitive way for reassurance before looking back at Mike. "Are you sure about that, Mike?"

Conveniently, the grounds of the cemetery were located on a hill, with the main building and its chapels built at the apex, and most of the graves on the slope. When there were downpours, the rain flowed naturally and freely down the path to the wrought iron gates at the entrance. So in the morning, while most of the ground was fresh, there were no signs of flooding. Quite the contrary. The grass was its usual lush green, and when the sun popped out for fleeting moments the sunlight would glisten off the dew.

After their third and final cup of tea they decided to do their rounds – a standard routine in which they inspected the grounds for litter or damage. Today was no exception, especially after the previous night's savage storm.

As they wandered over to the place where Mike had seen the fresh mound, it became obvious from a distance that indeed a fresh grave had been dug and then filled in. The crunching of the gravel underfoot stopped abruptly as the trio halted in unison just short of the grave. They looked across at each other wondering if they had forgotten it, or if perhaps it had been dug another day. But they knew that this particular area in the cemetery was part of the older grounds, and that no new graves were allowed, for it was designated as protected. Most new graves were organised way over in another section further down the hill.

After a short discussion they all concluded that the grave must have been dug the previous evening, after they had closed the grounds, and most likely during the violent storm.

"What do we do, Mike?" quizzed Joyce, while staring at the mound in front of them.

"Did either of you see anyone suspicious around this area yesterday?" asked Mike.

"I didn't!" said Joyce emphatically.

"Neither did I! But to be honest, people come and go, as you know," followed Colin.

"OK. Let's see now… Let me 'phone our regional office and see what the procedure is. I guess we'll have to go by the book. Never in all my years has this happened," said Mike, shaking his head in disbelief.

"Me neither," Joyce and Colin mumbled in unison.

All three stood in silence for a moment reflecting on what had been discovered in front of their very eyes.

"Bloody hell...? It's enormous! Now that's a huge and exceptionally long grave! Don't you think? Much longer than I've seen before. I want to take a closer look." Mike stood over the grave and realised that its length implied it was for a very tall body... very tall! Perhaps there had been an error in calculation.

"This would potentially be for a body well over 7ft tall at least. Oh my! I guess we may find out eventually what's going on. I'd better make that call..." Mike marched his way back to the office with Joyce and Colin following in his trail.

4. Soup and Evolution

It is the latter part of the 22nd Century and life still goes on, despite all the catastrophes that have come and gone, and of the Doomsday predictions that were laid out before us.

Dan sat at his favourite table by a window in a busy café near to his university with a college girl friend called Mich. He was eating a bowl of hot soup as Mich looked on while sipping her strong black coffee.

It was a relatively lively café that had a quirky retro look and feel about it, providing a perfect setting for the melange of music played by the hosts. The café perfectly shifted its ambience from the morning to mid-day and onward into the afternoon and evening. Often in the mornings the café would select classical music from the 19th Century to create a calmness. As lunchtime arrived, the music would become quite uplifting, and today they must be going through a '60s sound. Bizarre really, because even though it's the 22nd Century, the '60s sound derived from the 20th Century, and its name had stuck. If you wanted immortality, then be a famous musician! Currently they were playing The Beatles' debut single Love Me Do, initially released in 1962.

While technologies and fashions come and go, the staple diet and fundamentals of food and drink remain the same as in the centuries before us. Coffee and tea are still drunk in large quantities, while wine, beer and other alcoholic drinks are widely appreciated despite their effects on the human body. Even the wholesome soup, in an abundance of recipes, has been eaten for centuries and still thriving.

Dan was having an in-depth discussion with Mich about the beginning of life and the human race, and where we would be in the distant future. There was an incredible amount of information to take in as Dan's brain became fatigued with so much to understand about the human race. He held his head in his hands, with elbows on the table, to reflect. As he stared down into his round bowl of courgette soup, he was now wishing life would be just as simple, less demanding, less confusing, less complicated.

Dan's gaze became hazy as he focused into the deep pool of green soup, thinking how life had begun so long ago.

He started to tire, and from his fatigue his mind began to drift, viewing an image of a microscopic amoeba – a single-celled, free-living animal, a symbol for the beginning of life. In his image the amoeba was swimming in a pool of clear gel, as if examined under a laboratory microscope.

The amoeba is a creature with a single nucleus. It was first recorded way back in 1755 by August Johann Rösel von

Rosenhof. He named his discovery The Little Proteus, from the Greek god Proteus, god of the sea, rivers and bodies of water.

The amoeba proteus reproduces asexually through binary fission, where in the centre of the original cell forms two cells. The cell division results in two identical cells, or clones, because it reproduces asexually and so it simply copies its genetic information to the second cell. This entire process lasts anywhere from 30 minutes to an hour.

Under the right conditions a given group of amoeba can double its population in around 30 minutes. Because of the time gap between the generations, the amoeba can be observed for genetic and possibly evolutionary changes within the life span of a human.

The amoeba can be called immortal because it does not die due to natural death on its own, but continues its life through binary fission.

It is made of endoplasm and ectoplasm and is of science fiction itself...

Hunched over his soup, Dan thought of a single cell – no thoughts or worries, influenced by no-one, a little god, free to wander and reproduce at will, with no care in the world. If only it were that simple!

5. Story of Human History

Dan's friend Mich was attending UCL University in London, studying palaeoanthropology, anthropogeny and anthropology.

To Dan these subjects, apart from being long words, meant nothing, and so Mich felt obliged to explain them to him, hoping he would understand.

"Well, I know it sounds complicated, Dan, but really it's not... honestly. Palaeoanthropology is a branch of archaeology with a human focus. It seeks to understand the early development of anatomically modern humans.

"And then there's anthropogeny, which is the study of human origins. So, where did we come from?

"And finally there's anthropology. It studies the various aspects of humans within past and present societies... Have I confused you?" Mich questioned rhetorically, trying to express the differences between the subjects at the same time. Perhaps it was complicated after all...

Mich found all three subject matters incredibly fascinating due to the fact that Man was still discovering more on each subject. As more and more new discoveries were made, history books and the university's curriculum had to be re-written and this would continue to do so ad infinitum.

Dan just scratched his head. He had not realised that these subjects even existed! However, he understood there was a need for such studies, and they kind of made sense.

Mich gave Dan a quick lesson in human history as they sat at their regular table by the window in Quentin's Cappuccino, the local café.

It was rumoured the café was named after a previous owner who wanted to be an actor and film director. But he never really made it into show business, so he bought the coffee shop instead. Dan thought this was all pulp fiction, and probably the owner was just a film buff who had made a play on the words of a famous film director from the early 21st Century. Either way, the café had a catchy name, and it sounded pretty cool too. Both Mich and Dan loved the place. It was like a second home.

Dan and Mich had been friends now for over six months. They first met at a mutual friend's coming out party, and had been inseparable ever since.

Their favourite table stood in the corner, allowing them more privacy. They loved to sit there opposite each other, observing the daily traffic of people and vehicles passing by. They could be found there on most days, either when the full sunshine heated up their faces or when the sound of rain hit the window, giving them comfort as they sheltered from the miserable weather. They would be typically drinking their favourite tea or coffee, or a comforting hot chocolate drink on the freezing cold days.

The topic of the human race was not something which had ever really crossed Dan's mind, for he was studying art.

Dan's world of art was about shape and form, colour and shade, perspective and light. He would at times try to convey hidden messages and symbolism inside his creations, hoping in return that the observer would also conjure up their own feelings and interpretations of his work. He never really considered life other than in its beauty and pleasure. To him, life was a masterpiece in itself, and only artists could attempt to capture its beauty and complexities.

Dan now found the whole subject of human history intriguing. He especially enjoyed discussing it with Mich as she extrapolated the origins of Man from its very beginning. It was not about the beauty, but the design, and how Mankind had evolved over time… over a very long time.

"Is Earth really 4.5ish billion years old?" Dan asked as he stretched back on the red faux leather chair… and so Mich continued to explain while sitting opposite him with a smile on her face. It was a smile of contentment, revealing her pleasure in having someone at her side, interested in what she had to say, someone who gave her his full attention.

"It's not even possible to equate that timescale with our very own existence. From the original giant explosion at a point of singularity, as the current theory goes, with such puissance beyond our comprehension – to gaseous formations of stars and expulsion of dead stars given to planets of all guises – to other unknown entities, particles and dimensions.

"But once formed, that such selective and unique planets have the precise chemistry, opportune equations and events that would have progressed into the evolution of our very own existence... from a pool of soup," said Mich, as she gestured her hand towards Dan's bowl of hot soup. Dan stared down at his soup again as if to observe life's origins, and then he took another couple of spoonfuls as Mich continued to sip her coffee.

Then Mich began to explain about the future and what it had in store for humankind. She rapidly swung from the past and leapt ahead into the future, and what was ominously evident to come.

"What of Earth's future leading up to our Sun's final extinction 7.5 billion years from now, absorbing our Earth during the Sun's red giant phase?

"If you think what we have at the moment, with this so called global warming! Then imagine what it will be like four billion years from now with the increase in the Earth's surface temperature. This rise in temperature will cause a greenhouse effect from becoming closer to the Sun. It will lead to the extinction of all life on Earth!" concluded Mich. It was as if the pages of Earth's history and future were rapidly being flipped between a thumb and forefinger, gone! Dan stared at his soup transfixed as Mich snapped her fingers, "Gone!"

Mich and Dan sat and gazed at each other for a few moments while Dan soaked in all the information. There was much to comprehend. So much that he never realised was so relevant to the existence of our planet and the animal kingdom… and its unstoppable future.

Meanwhile outside it started raining again with the odd ray of sunshine through the café window onto their table. As the sunshine hit Dan's face, he lifted his head so as to soak up its radiance and pleasant warmth. Mich grinned, reflecting on the irony of discussing the sun just as it made a timely appearance on their table – a gentle reminder of its mighty presence.

Dan put his thoughts into perspective. "That really is such a long time isn't it? We really are talking about billions of years from now. Fortunately, I still have time to finish my soup," he quipped jokingly with a cheeky grin on his face.

"Dan, imagine… even if we were to talk about one million years, just think about that! If we based life expectancy to be around 100 years, then imagine how many generations of families of the human race would have existed in this period! Imagine the future evolution of Man," said Mich.

"What is the future evolution of Man?" inquired Dan as he looked Mich in the eye. How do you answer that, Mich asked herself.

Dan finished his soup, while Mich continued sipping what was left of her coffee. Dan wiped his mouth with his napkin and leaned back suitably nourished.

They both relaxed for a moment gazing out of the window, contemplating life and all its further mysteries waiting to unfold.

Do mysteries unfold or does Man unfold in order to create them?

6. Discovery

Mike and his team were relieved to make it back inside their warm office, protected from the cold and damp. He immediately headed to the computer. It was old, sluggish and in desperate need of an upgrade. It perched on an old wooden desk that was situated at the rear of the office together with a number of filing cabinets.

Colin had joked about the computer many a time. With a deadpan expression he would quip that it wouldn't be long before 'we have to bury it!' Yet another set of cemetery jokes added to his comedy repertoire.

Mike planned to have the computer replaced by the following year. He would need to arrange this at some point as December was approaching fast and he had some budget remaining in the current year – it was on his to-do list.

Neither Mike nor Joyce were computer wizards, and relied heavily on Colin to sort out any technical problems. However, they knew how to switch it on and how to log in. They also knew that if you had a problem, nine times out of ten, all you had to do was to switch it off and on again – even if it did wind up Colin a little. He said doing so could potentially corrupt files and 'kill' the system, whatever that meant.

Before calling his superiors, Mike decided to double check the team's itinerary on the computer. Perhaps it was all one huge mistake. But as the threesome checked together, with both Joyce and Colin overlooking Mike's shoulder, it was clear that there had been no error. They even searched to see if any paperwork had not been submitted or accidentally left in the in-tray, but after a while they found nothing.

They marched over to the garage to examine the digger. The machine had obviously not been touched, it was as dry as a bone and still clean from the previous day's maintenance. Even after returning to the grave and surveying the surrounding area they would have expected some tracks, especially after the wet stormy evening, but there was not a trace of anything remotely suspicious.

To dig a grave like that by hand would take hours, and with the digger maybe over 30 minutes. The thought of someone digging the grave and filling it in on an evening like last night was unbelievable, in fact it was complete madness.

They returned to the office and Mike immediately telephoned his regional office.

"You're going to have to contact your local police and take it from there," said the regional officer. "That's all you can do. I would assume that once the formalities are done with they will ask you to help them exhume the body. But you never know, I'm just guessing here.

"Let me know how you get on, Mike," he added. "Call me if you need any help, in fact call me anyway later, eh? I am really curious to see what happens. I've never had this happen before."

"No, neither have I, Len. Thanks for the help. And yes, we'll keep you posted, of course," replied Mike as he put down the 'phone.

Mike then telephoned his local police station and explained the circumstances. The on-duty officer proved to be efficient, noting all times and taking as many details as she could. "We'll send someone over, Mr. Stevens, and they'll advise you on what the procedure is. I'll give you an incident number anyway."

Sure enough, just over an hour passed when two uniformed police officers arrived at the cemetery. Within a short space of time Mike was presenting the grave to the officers. At the same time, he informed them that he and his colleagues believed it had been dug some time during the night when the grounds would have been locked.

When they had concluded, one of the two officers radioed into their station to explain the details further.

"If you don't mind, sir, we would like you to keep the grounds locked," requested one of the officers. "Our CID will have been notified. If you wait, we should be able to tell you when they will visit, sir."

It was already past 11am. Not much had been done in the way of normal duties. By now they would usually have been ready for their next tea break. But they didn't mind, for this distraction had actually made their daily routine slightly more interesting, albeit a little macabre.

Finally, they were on their next cup of tea and cake by the time a police car and van arrived in the grounds. Joyce wished she had baked more cake, or even perhaps a selection of cakes for all the visitors coming and going.

Three plain-clothed policemen stepped out of the car and approached Mike to shake hands. The senior officer introduced himself as Detective Sergeant Dawson, seemingly a middle aged man, almost reddish in the face and slightly balding, wearing a large heavy grey coat. Dawson introduced his colleagues as detective constables Braxton and Waites, who in contrast seemed quite young, healthy, slim and smartly dressed. The former was a ginger-haired man perhaps in his late 20s, while the other was a woman possibly a little younger with short, dark hair.

A squad of officers in white clothing filed out of the van raring for action, carrying equipment in readiness for digging and surveying the area.

A photographer had taken shots all around the grounds before the police arrived. But there had been little trace of note. No tracks, nor footprints… nothing! There were only Mike's footprints near the grave where he had encroached for a better look.

The area around the grave was cordoned off for the team of diggers to start excavating. However, before the excavation commenced, the team leader asked Mike to speak with his team and explain how the graves were made, including their typical depths, particularly in his cemetery. The whole operation had to be carried out with extreme caution, as they had no idea what would be found, or even how deep the grave really would be.

The digger carefully skimmed the surface so that it wouldn't break any potential objects as it progressed deeper into the hole. The soil was then placed to the side on a plastic sheet to protect the grass. It was a slow and arduous process and seemed to take forever.

After digging a metre deep it became apparent that they were reaching something.

Immediately the team leader shouted: "Stop! Drive the digger back!"

The leader turned to the rest of his team and told them to start using their trowels. It appeared as though there was no coffin, and so the team, as instructed, started to use small trowels to delicately remove the surrounding soil, which slowed the process down considerably more so.

After another 20 minutes, as the soil was carefully lifted, it became obvious there was an object covered in a soiled white cloth, its shape suggested a body, the size of which was enormous. Each officer and Mike had taken a second look. There was a certain disbelief, in fact they all eventually came to a stop, staring as the photographer took more shots. As the clicking of the camera ceased there was an air of nervousness. Even Mike, who was an experienced grave digger, could feel butterflies.

Despite the tense atmosphere and the levels of uncertainty, the team leader remained focused on his job and walked calmly over to DS Dawson and his colleagues to discuss the next step. Mike could only hear whispers as the team leader had his back to him and try as he might he couldn't make out anything of their conversation.

It didn't take too long to surmise that the body was at least 7ft tall and quite wide too, although it was difficult to follow its outline. It appeared to be dressed in a white cloth of a weird texture, a texture that reminded Mike of a cocoon with a spider's webbed cloth wrapped many times over.

The photographer finished taking his shots just as an ambulance arrived to transport the body to the crime laboratory.

Finally, after the team leader had finished his group conversation with Dawson, the cocoon was lifted by the digger with straps and delicately placed into the ambulance. At the same time, Mike and his team were asked to accompany young DC Braxton to the police station to give an account of the incident.

The ambulance drove calmly and quietly out of the cemetery, followed closely by the plain police car and van.

On leaving the cemetery Mike was asked to lock the gates behind them in order to secure the crime scene.

As the local church bells finished their chime, the cemetery grounds were now void of people and only the gravestones remained under the warmth of the sun. The only sound that could now be heard was a gentle breeze passing through the bushes and trees.

Peace and serenity had been restored.

7. Darwin's Theory

Dan and Mich drank their second coffee as he quizzed her more about the enigmatic evolution of Man.

"OK, Dan, let me tell you about a great man," started Mich. "A naturalist, who had a theory about evolution. His name was Charles Darwin, he lived through the 19th Century to a ripe old age of 73."

"It's a lovely theory really that looks into the biological evolution. It's a clever way to formulate a progression of our existence, based on a natural selection through the survival and reproduction of a species."

"There's a number of basic principles about this theory. It may be a bit difficult to follow... so don't worry if you become confused. But in principle Darwin starts by stating that more individuals are born with each generation that can survive – that certain traits of the individual are more attractive and susceptible to procreation than others – and those that are better suited to their environment will survive.

"But in essence he was saying that there is a natural selection going on as members of each generation pass their genes on to the next, and so on.

"However…." Mich paused and pointed her index finger in the direction of Dan, as if to suggest there was a slight anomaly, "and this is where Darwin's theory falls down a little – there's no complete evidence to back up his theory!

"So if you take, for example, the human species… there are huge gaps between each progression of our species. I'll show you them in a minute. But it's these gaps that leave so many unsolved questions relating to evolution."

"It makes you wonder if Darwin's theory can't be 100 per cent true until these gaps or missing links are resolved. Why did these new species appear? And why is there no evidence to help us understand where they came from… or developed from?" Mich paused, as if not sure how to conclude her understanding of Darwin's theory. It was as if she really hadn't understood why the gaps had occurred.

"OK. So where does this Darwin's evolution start?" asked Dan.

"Well, without going into too much depth – you have to understand that there's a whole course syllabus on this stuff, so I can't tell you everything over a cup of coffee!

"However, the history of life on Earth began about 3.8 billion years ago, initially with single-celled cells, such as bacteria," continued Mich.

"Then, multicellular life evolved over a billion years later. It's only in the last 570 million years that the kind of life forms we are familiar with began to evolve, starting with arthropods such as the spider family, centipedes, crabs and lobster species. The arthropods were followed by fish 530 million years ago (Ma), then land plants 475 Ma and forests 385 Ma. We are mammals, and we didn't evolve until 200 Ma!"

Mich put it into simple words: "Our own species, Homo sapiens, arrived only 200,000 years ago. So we humans have only been around for a mere blip of the Earth's history."

Dan tried to summarise: "OK, so what you are saying is that based on Darwin's theory we couldn't have just appeared, right? I mean, what exactly happened about 200,000 years ago?" Dan's face contorted as if trying to comprehend …

"Did humans just pop on to the planet?" quizzed Dan.

"You're saying that evolution is a gradual existence, a slow progression of inherited traits?" Dan was trying to interpret the rules of Darwin's theory.

"So way back 200,000 years ago, was there all of a sudden a tribe of new humans, with a number of females and males in order to start and continue the race? Did they just pop up out of nowhere? Hey presto!" Asked Dan naively as Mich shrugged her shoulders in response.

8. Human Species

Mich tried to explain to Dan that documentation identifying the stages of the human race is based on Darwin's evolution theory of natural selection, rather than having been created out of nothing.

However, even she had to admit that the evidence so far had failed to support the evolution from ape to Man, or any other type of macroevolution. It was all due to the fact that there was a lack of proof, through the complete absence of transitional fossils. In fact the fossil record shows all life forms appearing fully formed and not changing during their period on Earth, except for monumental extinctions such as the dinosaurs.

"OK, so where does the human race begin and how does it continue throughout history up to today?" Dan seemed to really have a hunger for the incredible story of Man's existence.

Mich opened up her laptop and pulled up a demo which gave an excellent presentation of the history of Man's evolution. "Believe it or not, it begins millions of years ago …"

"Can you believe that 4.4 million years ago there was a human species called Ardipithecus ramidus – its fossil was discovered in the late 20th Century. He was 4ft tall and bipedal – that's having two feet, Dan! It's thought that they lived as forest dwellers.

"Then came another new species called Australopithecus anamensis between 4.2 and 3.9 million years ago. They were named in 1995 when their bones were found in Kenya. They showed advanced bipedal features, but their skulls closely resembled the ancient apes.

"Let's see now, who came next?" said Mich, searching through her list. "Oh yes, then came another species called Australopithecus afarensis around 3.9 to three million years ago. They had ape-like faces with sloping foreheads, ridges over their eyes, flat noses and chinless lower jaws. They were about 3ft 6in to 5ft tall and again they were fully bipedal. Seems the thickness of their bones showed that they were quite strong. Their overall build was similar to a human although the head and face were proportionately much larger."

"Are you bored yet, Dan?" enquired Mich, aware that this was quite heavy stuff to go through for an art student.

"No, not at all, in fact I am curious to see how we evolved through the species… that's if we did evolve?"

"Erm, well yes, we did! Otherwise we'd still be grunting and dragging our knuckles on the floor," said Mich jokingly, and both Dan and Mich started to laugh.

"OK, so who's next? Ah yes, the Australopithecus africanus about three million to two million years ago. These were similar to the previous species, the afarensis, they were bipedal with a slightly larger body. Their brain was not advanced enough for speech, and the shape of their jaw was human-like. They were herbivores and ate tough, hard-to-chew plants."

"There were two more species of the Australopithecus and they were robustus and bosei ranging from two million to 1.5 million years ago and 2.1 to 1.1 million years ago. The boisei was smaller than the robustus whilst the robustus was similar to the africanus but with larger skulls and teeth. They had no indication of speech capabilities. Some say that these two were in fact of the same species.

"Then came the Homo species, starting with Homo habilis around 2.4 to 1.5 million years ago. When they discovered his fossil remains they also found many tools, which gave him the nickname of The Handy Man. The brain shape showed evidence that some speech had developed. It is believed he was about 5ft tall and weighed around 100 pounds.

"Not many to go now, Dan! These Homo species seemed to develop much quicker than their Australopithecus predecessors, they had better communication skills and a good use of tools."

"Keep going, I haven't dropped off yet!" smiled Dan in response.

"OK, but I'm hoping you may have heard of the next set who were more like modern Man. There was the Homo erectus some 1.8 million to 300,000 years ago. As I say, this species was similar to modern Man, in his case his brain was the same size and he could definitely speak. It was only his head and face that differed.

"He developed tools, weapons, fire and even learned to cook his food. How about that then, Dan?!" Mich nodded her head as Dan himself started to nod in appreciation of a major development in our evolution. "They travelled out of Africa and into China and Southeast Asia developing clothing for northern climates. Eventually they turned to hunting for food.

"Then came three species of Homo sapiens.

"The first was Homo sapien archaic from 500,000 to 200,000 years ago, he spoke and his main characteristics were such that he had a rounded skull with smaller features. His skeleton shows he had a stronger build than modern humans, but was well proportioned.

"Then came Homo sapien neanderthalensis some 150,000 to 35,000 years ago. He lived in Europe and Southwest to Central Asia. His brain size was average but larger than modern Man. However his head was shaped differently, kind of longer and lower. His nose was large too and extremely different from modern Man in structure. He was about 5ft 6in tall with a heavy skeleton that showed attachments for massive muscles. He was far stronger than modern Man, and his jaw was massive with a receding forehead like erectus."

Finally, Mich, in trying to keep Dan entertained, impersonated a magician with an act of bravado…. "Dah dahhh… And so our own species arrived, the Homo sapiens, approximately 120,000 years ago, and in the scheme of things we are not that old, really!"

"But Mich," said Dan, "As I keep asking, are you telling me that each stage has a different species? How does that work? I mean how does the next stage arrive from almost nowhere? What happens during the gaps between each race? It's almost like someone is tweaking with the model, trying to upgrade, don't you think?" said Dan as he raised his arms out to his sides offering his hands up to the air.

"I see what you mean. Well they say they have yet to find the missing links, but even with these gaps the transition must be so marginal. It's like a person not realising they are growing in height, it's not until you measure and look back that you see the differences." Mich was trying to make it easy for Dan to understand, although she did agree with his arguments.

"Well another theory would be that each evolution occurred in different parts of the world, so in some way they arrived in time from a different path of progression. It's much in the same way that something must have happened when the chimp's evolution separated from that of the humans, as they both descended from the ape, so it is said." Mich sat back in her chair.

"I'm a bit sceptical, Mich. Perhaps I'm too much into conspiracy theories. But it's almost like we're being reprogrammed in order to improve the species.... Crazy, I know, but it makes logical sense." Dan tapped with his index finger against his temple, in a way to suggest there was something going on that we didn't know about.

"Come on, Dan – that's just ridiculous, and you know it! Even if it is interesting to see how we all view the human race!" Mich had a smile on her face as she teasingly leaned forward and dug her hand into his ribs.

9. Pathology

Since the discovery of the mysterious cocoon in the grave, DS Dawson had been unusually full of anxiety, somehow managing to keep his thoughts to himself. He could not comprehend what he had just witnessed. It was beyond all reason, and most definitely unusual. Perhaps it was something out of this world, even though this idea seemed utterly ridiculous. He had to think rationally. He was a quiet, thoughtful man. A man of logic. And in this case, he just couldn't fathom it out.

He was a polite and mildly spoken man, with a good work ethic, and had a vast amount of experience as a detective. It was no surprise that he therefore had the respect of his team of detective constables.

He was a man in his early 50s, already grey and thin on top, and was around an average 5ft 7ins tall. Somehow though, in his appearance he looked shorter, which was probably due to his round figure, caused by a lack of exercise as well as a love of food and wine. Although he never discussed it with his team, they knew he was married and had two adult children who had left the nest.

It was just after 3pm when Dawson took a 25-minute drive across to the other side of town from his office. He was going to meet George, the crime pathologist, in her laboratory to discuss the process of identifying the body uncovered at the cemetery.

After the dry early morning sunshine, rain had been pouring down all day. Dawson had his windscreen wipers on throughout the entire journey, cursing the miserable weather and wishing for the summer to arrive. He had been visiting the lab for a number of years now, so he knew the route like the back of his hand. He may as well have been blindfolded, for sometimes he would reach his destination without remembering any part of the journey. He parked in close proximity to the laboratory building and ran across into the warm and dry entrance, arriving out of breath.

Dawson met George in her small but well organised office. This was quite typical before they'd move on to the adjacent lab, as George always liked to offer a coffee or tea, and to discuss the agenda or the needs of her guest. Dawson was quite familiar to this routine, especially after a good many years of visiting George. He always went along with it, even though at times his schedule was too hectic to accommodate this kind gesture. However, today Dawson needed a hot drink to warm up, so he sat down with George for a cup of tea and a couple of chocolate biscuits – his favourite.

"Still raining out there! I have to admit I'm getting a little bit fed up with this recent weather. When's it going to stop?" asked Dawson.

"Yes, well there's been a lot of that lately. Blame it on global warming, that's what I say!" answered George.

"And how's the family, George?"

"Oh not too bad, Dawson, many thanks. I trust yours are all well?" she replied, and they went on to discuss the recently discovered body.

"Right then… so what have you brought me this time? I have to admit this one's a good 'un. Certainly has made my day, I have to say. Makes a change from the usual mundane corpses, don't you think?" George spoke rhetorically. It was their typical idle chit-chat and dry humour. There was nothing wrong with exchanging certain pleasantries during the professional day.

"Yes, I thought you might say that. I must admit I'm really curious to see what you find out… We don't really have much evidence to go on at the moment, George – no possessions, no tracks… nothing!" said Dawson.

"In fact…it's been quite a strange one, really. We've never seen this type of body before. I mean the way it's been encased in some type of webbed cloth, very bizarre!" continued Dawson.

George nodded in empathy for her colleague, "Yes, you're not wrong there, hopefully all will be revealed when we go to the lab and open it up."

They drank their beverages and wandered over to the laboratory, which was just down the corridor. This was Dawson's first chance to understand the details surrounding the condition of the body, and to study any examination results that may shed light on how and when the death occurred. He had considered whether to bring Braxton to the lab, but decided to see what he was dealing with first, before including his colleague in the case.

As expected, the lab was practically empty except for a couple of steel tables and storage drawers for corpses. All the walls and the ceiling were a mundane blank white, as you would expect in any hospital. The room was incredibly cold, it always had been since Dawson could remember, and so he decided to keep his jacket on for the process, whereas George was in her usual robe, hat and rubber gloves – the standard costume, as she would jokingly call it.

There was a very macabre atmosphere inside the laboratory, as to be expected, with a real sense and smell of death, of rotting flesh that overpowered any odour of disinfectant. George and Dawson had had a number of incidents in the past where new CID recruits had suffered from sickness on their first visit. It requires a strong stomach to overcome the bad odour, and a mentality to switch off from death and any autopsy procedures that a pathologist undertakes. Dawson was by now a seasoned professional and had gone beyond any sensitivity, except for the chill in the room. George had once even joked with him that the laboratory assistants kept their milk in one of the body storage units, and Dawson had quite believed her, knowing how these assistants had a dark sense of humour.

George and Dawson patiently watched in silence as the laboratory assistants laid the corpse out on to a steel table. They both stood either side, looking down on the cocooned body in amazement, both wondering what they would eventually discover. The table was found to be just sufficient in size to cater for such an overly large corpse. Normally the body would have been covered with a white cloth, but this case was highly unusual due to the fact that it was already wrapped in a cloth, giving an appearance of a mummy from an Egyptian tomb.

"Well, Dawson, I have to say this really is a new one for the books. It's the first time I've had an Egyptian mummy in my lab!" George said jokingly. But she soon realised that Dawson hadn't seen the funny side, as he remained focused with his eyes glued to the cocoon.

In general, Dawson was quite a serious person; perhaps it was his older age or his way of behaving in his senior role. Both George and Braxton steered away from any jokes when it came to conversing with Dawson, more as a matter of respect than anything else.

They stood motionless for a fleeting moment as George took a deep breath, almost as if to trap her butterflies. "OK, Dawson, here goes, let's see what's inside this monster." She picked up a surgical scalpel.

Slowly and delicately George started to make an incision in the white cloth where she believed the head was located. The wrapping appeared to be fairly easy to penetrate with no extra effort required by the pathologist.

She then worked her way down the centre of the corpse with a sharp scalpel, stopping for a fleeting moment as she checked Dawson's demeanour. He looked on with complete fixation, as though in a trance, as she continued to cut, but this time with surgical scissors. Both were holding their breath in anticipation.

George had only cut along by half a metre when whatever was inside the cloth – inside this cocoon – caused both Dawson and George to freeze in total disbelief.

They shot a look at each other in complete shock. This case had taken another twist, and was becoming more and more unusual and sinister. Dawson didn't like it, neither did George. What on earth was going on?

10. Descended From Apes

Dan was finally a little overwhelmed. He found the whole explanation of the evolution of the human race heavy going. So many different species to remember. It wasn't just that; it was also the comprehension of how they varied from each other and how they could possibly start from seemingly out of nowhere. Where or why were there missing links?

But he was determined to persist in trying to understand it all. He ordered another two cups of coffee and continued: "OK, so I guess the big question is… in the very beginning of our human species, were we really descended from apes?"

Mich was ready for this question "Well, the chimpanzee and another ape, the bonobo, are humans' closest living relatives. For a clear understanding of how closely they are related, scientists compare their DNA, an essential molecule that has the instruction manual for building each species.

"Humans and chimps share a surprising 98.8 per cent of their DNA. So humans, chimps and bonobos descended from a single ancestor that lived six or seven million years ago.

"As humans and chimps gradually evolved, their DNA passed from generation to generation with a number of mutations.

At the same time, with many of these DNA changes, differences developed between human and chimp appearance and behaviour.

"Human and chimp DNA is nearly identical when you compare the bands on their chromosomes – these are the bundles of DNA inside nearly every cell.

"The weirdest part is that there are two Chromosomes 2 in a chimp, whereas in humans the same two chromosomes 2s are fused together – a perfect illustration of a mutation.

"Human and chimp X chromosomes both contain about 1,100 different genes or sets of instructions," explained Mich. "Each gene affects a particular trait in the body and a great example is the OPN1LW gene which affects how we perceive red colour vision."

She continued: "Most genes in humans and chimps are nearly identical and both have the OPN1LW gene, but mice don't, and so they have trouble seeing red." Mich was starting to worry that she may have lost Dan with so much technical information to understand.

"You know Mich, it's almost like the DNA, chromosomes and genes are like a set of computer programs for the body," Dan said. "Are you saying, as an example, that we have a sub-program called OPN1LW that lets us see red? Wow! And that our brains are like computer processors with memory?

Do our brains shut down at night when we sleep? And then do our brains re-boot when we wake up?

"And as for that Chromosome 2 business. Well, that sounds very much like someone just came along and fused it with a blowtorch! A very sophisticated one at that, I imagine!" Dan added in a down-to-earth manner.

"Hmmmm, I suppose you could say that, couldn't you!" Mich replied with a chuckle and a loving gaze towards Dan.

11. Love and War

Wanting more, Dan was now curious to know what happened next. "OK… so then what about us? What about our current species, did you say… Homo sapiens?"

"Well… the current theory is that modern Man originally came from Africa due to the onset of the last Ice Age, migrating around 60,000 years ago through Eurasia when the Neanderthals and Denisovans were still in existence. The Denisovans were a close relation to the Neanderthals, although they are thought to go back as far as 400,000 years ago.

"Interbreeding took place between the Homo sapiens, Neanderthals and Denisovans. As a result of this finding, DNA from the Neanderthals or Denisovans exists in modern Man today, with three per cent to five per cent in Aboriginal Australians.

"Everyone living outside Africa has approximately one per cent to two per cent of Neanderthal in them, except the indigenous sub-Saharan Africans who have none, as their ancestors did not migrate through Eurasia.

"The great mystery in anthropology is why did the Neanderthals become extinct approximately 30,000 years ago, just at the same time as the Homo sapiens arrived in Eurasia…?" asked Mich rhetorically.

"The conclusion was that they either made love, or war... or both!" she added.

"Actually, you know what Mich? I was just thinking... If all this evolution stuff is still correct, then has it ever occurred to you that my ancestor... and yours.... were walking this planet wearing loin cloths and living in caves? All this, during the Stone Age or even beyond that! It's something I've never really thought about until now! I wonder if he looked like me?" said Dan with a wink.

"Ha ha ha...yes, maybe he was one of those who did the cave drawings! The ones with the craniums," joked Mich.

"Very funny, ha ha!" replied Dan, as they laughed together.

"Well it's true what you say about our very ancient ancestors, Dan. But for them to look similar to you or me is even harder to imagine, particularly when you see the profiles of the Stone Age men with their large foreheads."

"So, Dan, here's another thing to think about... Not only did our generations of ancestors manage to survive all the catastrophes of our planet, but did you also know that the odds of both you and I being conceived during sex are huge?

"When you think of all the generations before our time... Just the odds against your birth are immense – when you analyse the battle of the semen racing towards the egg during conception, and the winners were you and me!

In one conception there are approximately 40 million to possibly 1.2 billion sperm, each racing to be the one that fertilises the egg! It's incredible isn't it?" prompted Mich.

"Yes, I guess we should feel privileged to even be here, especially with those odds over who knows how many generations," concluded Dan.

They realised that time was moving on, and that they had better get going, for they both had lectures to attend.

They drank up and left the café suitably fed and watered – or rather fed and coffeed.

12. Shock

The deathly silence in the crime lab seemed to last for several minutes, although in reality it must have been only seconds. Both Dawson and George looked at each other for answers, but neither of them were sure what to say.

The evidence was there for all to see! For there... inside the soiled cloth... inside this webbed cocoon, were two bodies! Both corpses were well over 7ft tall. George also remarked on the fact that strangely there was hardly any smell emanating from the opening in the cut.

"Oh my, Dawson, I don't like the look of this at all. It's highly irregular. There's hardly any odour, and that would be the first thing I would expect, let alone the fact that there are two bodies in here! Where the hell did they come from?" George was frowning, highly stressed, and giving Dawson a side glance.

Dawson felt a little awkward and embarrassed, yet he knew it was not his fault that these corpses were in this lab. However, he did realise that he had better give George some space to let her focus on what was evidently no ordinary autopsy. "I think I'd better leave you to it, George. Seems you have your hands full here. Please come over to my office when you're done. Take your time, there's no hurry." Dawson spoke softly knowing that George must be feeling stressed at such an unusual discovery. George nodded in acknowledgement as she continued to concentrate, not daring to blink as she finished cutting open the cocoon.

Before Dawson left the lab he had made a number of observations about the couple. He was no pathologist, but he knew what he had witnessed, and as he left he was trying to formulate a simple explanation.

Dawson left the building and stopped just outside the entrance under the canopy, away from the rain. He stood motionless for a moment to gather his thoughts, contemplate his observations, and appreciate the clean air, especially after the bad odour in the lab. He looked up at the sky, searching for inspiration. "Now, what do we do?" he asked himself.

Sometimes in stressful moments like this, he felt like taking up smoking again, but knew it was a disgusting habit, so he took out a mint and popped it into his mouth for comfort.

The whole episode was very odd and strange indeed. So he left George to continue her job while he returned to the station to discuss the recent events with Braxton. It was time to get Braxton more involved in the case – a younger, fresher blood.

Meanwhile, back at the police station, Mike, Joyce and Colin each gave individual accounts of the moment they discovered the grave. Each signed their short statements accordingly. All three left the station and returned to the cemetery.

They were told to keep the cemetery locked at all times until further notice and not to approach the grave which had been cordoned off by the police.

None of them were given any information about the discovered body, so all they could do was speculate among themselves. They were told they would be updated as and when necessary, and would be advised about when they could re-open the grounds in due course.

Once they were back at the cemetery, Mike telephoned the regional office to explain the events of the day. He promised to keep his bosses informed. He also printed off a notice and posted it on the gates. The notice explained why the grounds were temporarily closed and gave a contact number for any emergencies. The explanation was fairly generic, stating that the grounds were under standard maintenance.

It was close to the end of the day and there was not really enough time to start any new tasks. So they all finished early. They would have plenty to tell their families as it had been a rather unforgettable, dramatic, and at times very stressful day.

13. Pyramids and Star Constellations

Joe Braxton was the younger brother of DC Richard Braxton by seven years. He was still at college studying computing and was very much a geek. He shared the same light ginger hair as Richard, but whilst Richard's hair was short, Joe's was long and bushy, and perhaps a little unkempt. He was not quite a hippie, but very easily recognised as a student in his jeans and T-shirts or sweaters.

Since his early childhood Richard had always been called by his surname. For some reason that name had stuck, some said it was because there were too many Richards in his school class. However, Joe was just 'Joe', for there couldn't be two Braxtons. During his younger years there had been a few attempts at Jo-Joe or sometimes JJ, referring to his middle name, John. Of course, when his mother or father had been angry with him, there had been the odd occasion where he'd been called Joseph. His college buddies nicknamed him Joe 90 after a Gerry Anderson character created in the 1960s, especially when Joe was wearing his black rimmed reading glasses. Mostly, he liked just plain old 'Joe'.

It was late and, as usual, Joe was on the internet. It was his favourite pastime. There was no greater comfort than spending hour after hour searching and looking for any new material which supported his numerous theories.

In this world Joe could discover anything and everything. He could stretch his mind to all extremes and magically arrange all the pieces together. He adored puzzles and the discovery of the unknown. To him, life was one enormous puzzle waiting to be solved. Some people would accept that it is what it is, whilst for others, like Joe, they feel a desire to understand it.

Locked in his study with the room light switched off and only the beam from his computer screen engulfing his face, Joe's eyes were transfixed on the latest photos from outer-space. Images from our moon, Mars and beyond, images that possibly conveyed unnatural structures, could this be possible?

He loved the old science fiction movies of bygone days, from the totally believable to the incredibly bizarre.

One of his favourite movies was the original The Day the Earth Stood Still, made way back in 1951. It explained a concept, a future scenario that Joe felt was a real possibility.

Another film that conjured up all possibilities in the same way was his other favourite, The War of the Worlds, by H. G. Wells, made in 1953. Although the original novel was written way back in 1897 it is incredible to think that someone in the latter part of the 19th Century could imagine such an Earth shattering event from outer-space.

These movies, along with his fascination for conspiracies, meant Joe was forever formulating all sorts of conjectures – all of which to him were perfectly viable in his real world.

Joe flipped his screen to his latest theme.

He was always fascinated by the latest updates on ancient buildings and geometries found on Earth. The latest expert opinions were such that it often meant their history stretched to way earlier than previously thought. He believed the theories, they had to be true, this made sense to him as it solved one of his riddles.

One of his initial findings had led him on a journey of discovery regarding the pyramids on Earth.

The strange fascination about the pyramids is that no-one has a clue as to why or how they were constructed. What function did they provide to humanity – that's if they were for humanity? And why a pyramid? Why not a cube or dome? Was the pyramid the final solution after a long history of trial and error? The historians had their hypothesis, but Joe thought they hadn't a clue, no real idea as to the reason for their existence.

The most commonly known pyramids are of course the ones in Giza, Cairo, Egypt – the Great Pyramid, supposedly constructed in c. 2560-2540 BC, along with the smaller Pyramid of Khafre and the modest-sized Pyramid of Menkaure.

Apart from the standard theory that the pyramids were tombs, new theories started to emerge. One proposition was that they were in fact sonic resonators feeding off the frequency of Earth in order to generate power. There was even evidence within the pyramids to support this notion. Electrodes and minerals were found in certain chambers that could be used in the chemical production of hydrogen and a chamber that would amplify the frequencies.

Not far from the pyramids are the large stone boxes at the Serapeum of Saqqara. These boxes were previously assumed to be coffins for the Apis bull – an animal considered to be both a deity and a manifestation of the pharaohs. However, no evidence of any such animals were found inside them; no skeletons nor remnants of food or artefacts. According to the latest theory they were in fact giant capacitors or large scale batteries. Hieroglyphics on carved stone illustrated Egyptians carrying large light bulbs – so this was not so ridiculous after all.

Along with these major monuments is a number of smaller satellite edifices, known as the Queens' Pyramids, causeways and valley pyramids. Some even say that there is an underground river running beneath the pyramid complex.

The arrangement of the pyramids is a representation of the Orion constellation lined up as of approximately 12,000 years ago, which, when one starts looking into other countries' pyramids, becomes quite relevant to the civilisations that built them.

An example of other civilisations building pyramids lies in Mexico, located about 30 miles or 50 kilometres north east of modern-day Mexico City. Teotihuacan was one of the largest urban centres in the ancient world. It has three large pyramids that are also in the formation of Orion's Belt. Teotihuacan was given its name by the Aztecs. It means the place where the gods were created. The three pyramids are the Pyramid of the Moon, Pyramid of the Sun and Pyramid of Quetzalcoatl, which was a feathered serpent god. The distance between these sites in Egypt and Mexico is over 20,500 kilometres, nearly 13,000 miles away.

The Pyramids of China, located around the Chinese city of Xi'an, are even more fascinating for a number of reasons. The Great Pyramid of Egypt has around a 52,900 square metre footprint, yet the Great Pyramid of China has been claimed to have a staggering 202,000 square metre footprint, almost four times the size of the one in Cairo. Plus, according to reports, numerous European excursions managed to take samples of objects and metals from around the Pyramids of China. Analysis showed that these structures could be well over 8,000 years old. Not only that but interestingly the metallic material found at the Pyramids has not been identified, since it is made out of materials unknown to modern science.

The other more commonly-known pyramids are in Peru. But after many years of searching it became obvious that pyramids existed throughout our planet.

The list of ancient pyramids spans the globe, from the famous pyramids of Egypt, to Mesoamerican pyramids, Chinese tomb pyramids, South American step pyramids, Mesopotamian ziggurats, North American mound pyramids and even Roman ceremonial pyramids. These ancient structures pop up across the globe right through the centuries in cultures which often have no connection to one another.

These discoveries then raised questions about who built the pyramids and why they were constructed in the first place. How could such technology be commonly known and built across the whole world? This would need a universal communication with one common goal. The question is who were these people, and what was their connection during that period?

Incredibly, a pyramid on the far side of Earth's moon in the Ryder crater was discovered....

But then, in 1976, when the Viking 1 spacecraft was circling the planet Mars, it spotted the shadowy likeness of a human face. An enormous head nearly two miles from end to end appeared to be staring back at the cameras from a region of the Red Planet called Cydonia Mensa – and then, just five kilometres away, a gigantic pyramid structure was also observed!

14. Older than thought

Joe continued to delve deeper into the Egyptian pyramids and their guardian sphinx. According to a study presented at the International Conference of Geoarchaeology and Archaeomineralogy the enigmatic and mysterious sphinx of Egypt is around 800,000 years old. This proves that there is very little knowledge about our actual history, which is more mysterious and surprising than the mainstream scholars suggest.

The Great Sphinx of Egypt is an ancient construction that has baffled researchers through the ages. Carved from a single block of stone, no one has been able to date it accurately. This is due to there being no written records or mentions in the past.

The new theory regarding the age of the sphinx is based upon geological studies which suggest that it pre-dates everything we know about Ancient Egypt and history.

The belief is that the sphinx was submerged for a long time under water and, to support this hypothesis, scholars look towards geological studies of the Giza Plateau. According to these studies at the end of the Pliocene geologic period (between 5.2 and 1.6 million years ago), seawater entered the Nile Valley and gradually created flooding in the area. This led to the formation of lacustrine deposits which are 180 metres above the present level of the Mediterranean Sea.

This mysterious dating of the sphinx forces one to ask that if the enigmatic monument is in fact 800,000 years old as the geological study suggests, then who built it, bearing in mind we are talking nearly one million years ago? Are we looking at evidence that points to the existence of an unknown intelligent civilisation in history? Is it possible that an advanced ancient race of people inhabited the Giza Plateau in the distant past, before the creation of the Ancient Egyptian civilisation as we know it? And if this culture did develop on the shores of today's River Nile… is it possible that other advanced civilisations developed elsewhere on our planet hundreds of thousands of years ago?

The sphinx could have existed since the days of the followers of Horus, a race of pre-dynastic and semi-divine beings, which, according to the beliefs of the Ancient Egyptians had ruled thousands of years before the pharaohs of Egypt.

The Inventory Stella was found at Giza by Auguste Mariette in the 1850s, in the ruins of the Temple of Isis. The Stella clearly states that Khufu restored the sphinx. This points to the fact that the sphinx was constructed much before Khufu and not by him as some had suggested.

The Stella reads:

"*Long live The King of Upper and Lower Egypt, Khufu, given life*
He found the house of Isis, Mistress of the Pyramid, by the side of
the hollow of Hwran (The sphinx)
and he built his pyramid beside the temple of this goddess and he
built a pyramid for the King's daughter Henutsen beside this
temple.
The place of Hwran Horemakhet is on the South side of the House
of Isis, Mistress of the pyramid
He restored the statue, all covered in painting, of the guardian of
the atmosphere, who guides the winds with his gaze.
He replaced the back part of the Nemes head-dress, which was
missing with gilded stone
The figure of this god, cut in stone, is solid and will last to eternity,
keeping its face looking always to the East."

15. Another Sphinx?

And then… just when all the mysteries of the sphinx had become more and more analysed, with all its possible history and phases explained… just when the conclusion of its existence was unique, another sphinx appears on the horizon.

Approximately 250 kilometres away from Karachi, along the Makran coastline of Southern Balochistan in Pakistan, within the Hingol National Park lies the Balochistan Sphinx.

It's incredible to think that this magnificent architectural jewel only became known around 2004 when new routes were opened up along the coast.

The theory is that the sphinx belongs to a temple complex including steps, niches, pillars and symmetries on the site, although at the moment no official archaeological examinations have taken place in the region. It appears as though the sphinx is protecting the temple in the same way the Egyptian sphinx is protecting the pyramids.

Joe came to the same conclusion as the many scholars who analysed the evidence on the sphinx. Although perhaps it was not necessarily a conclusion, but ultimately more of a question – how did these civilisations construct similar monuments when they are so distant from each other, in this case the distance from Balochistan, Pakistan, to Giza, Egypt is just over 4,500 km.

16. First Examination

Dawson returned to his office both mentally and physically exhausted, and immediately went over to the coffee machine to grab himself a drink, not saying a word to anyone. Braxton and Waites watched him in silence as he appeared to be in his own little world, deep in thought. They knew best to leave him alone and had their own work to deal with anyway. However, they were certain that when Dawson was ready he would open up a little to them.

After opening and closing some drawers aimlessly and finally launching his computer, Dawson pulled back his chair and called Braxton in to his office. There was no idle chit-chat, nor pleasantries, as Dawson was almost frowning, concentrating on what he would say to Braxton. Immediately Dawson started to discuss with Braxton what he witnessed in the lab.

"Sit down please, Braxton," said Dawson as he waited for him to settle.

"What I have to say to you… is that today has been a rather unusual and unexpected day. What I saw with George in her lab was quite mind blowing. I still can't quite fathom it. Never have I come across such a situation like this in my entire career. It's beyond normal… and so I am trying to rationalise what I saw. So bear with me… OK?" Dawson seemed to want to qualify what he was about to say to Braxton, and at the same time Braxton could see that Dawson was a little shaken up.

"Braxton… the first thing I need to tell you is that this cocoon and its wrapping was opened up by George… and we discovered two bodies inside!" Dawson glanced at Braxton for a reaction. "I don't know who was more surprised, myself or George. But I have to say it took my breath away, and George's, as you can imagine."

"Bloody hell, Sarge! That's not what I expected either. Mind you… I'm not sure what I did expect to be honest. It's very strange, what on earth is going on?" Braxton shifted in his chair with unease and a look of shock on his face.

"From what I saw… they were both bald, clean… and pale as you would expect from any dead body, but they were almost a pure white – with no blemishes. They were almost angelical, almost identical, almost asexual and although I can't describe it, I understood that one was a male and the other, female. Yet I can't understand why I would think that." Dawson spoke almost in a disbelieving manner, with a puzzled look on his face, as if he were wincing. "And the other bizarre thing was that, apart from the fact they were in the same wrapping, they were holding hands as a couple would do so," concluded Dawson.

"Wow, this is really mind-blowing. Not sure what to say, Sarge. I can tell from the way in which you describe it, it's all highly irregular and bizarre as you say. Are you OK, Sarge? I can see that it has affected you." Braxton noticed that Dawson looked tired and somewhat stressed.

"Yes, Braxton, you could say that it was quite emotional, as George opened up the cocoon to see a loving couple in death, holding hands together. I felt that we had disturbed something very personal and private – that they would have been laid to rest in peace and yet there we were digging them up again," concluded Dawson quite solemnly.

Braxton looked down at the floor in a reflecting manner, thinking that Dawson may be quite right in his analysis. Braxton then wondered how many other bodies had been dug up in the past and placed in museums away from their original resting place. Tutankhamun, an Egyptian pharaoh of the 18th dynasty, immediately sprung to mind.

It was starting to get late and Braxton looked outside the office window, it had already become quite dark outside, and the fatigued Dawson was close to calling it a day.

Braxton had now been brought up to date with the details of the case. He wanted to lift Dawson out of his melancholy, and at the same time he was also keen to find out if there was any news on the two dead bodies. "Come on, Sarge, let's give George a call, she must have finished by now, don't you think?"

"Maybe, Braxton, but this is a very strange case. I wouldn't be surprised if she hasn't concluded her examination. There is obviously something very irregular about the whole affair. But let's see, she won't be long," said Dawson.

On cue, there was a knock at the door and George entered the room, also feeling a little tired and looking forward to going home.

"Well?!" Dawson and Braxton eagerly cried out.

"OK, well I'm glad you're sitting down chaps because you're not going to believe me.... they're both over 7ft tall..." replied George.

"I guessed that, George; that was the first thing that hit me! But what else is there?" demanded Dawson.

"They are both unblemished, I mean there's not one scar on either of them. Everyone has a scar, right? Not one! Their anatomy is almost perfect but... well... there is no body hair, ... no body hair... I thought at first that maybe they had been shaved, perhaps just before burial, but while there are pores ... there is no hair.... no hair... well... and..."

"Come on, George, what is it?"

"Well, the male's genitals are very small, very small indeed, just odd considering the guy is over 7ft tall. The female... well I say female, as the anatomy suggests female. I will need a second opinion, but… well… there are genitalia but no internal reproductive organs, and I can't see any evidence of surgery. I am at a complete loss."

"You look exhausted George, you should get an early night and sleep on it," remarked Dawson.

"I think all of us could do with an early night chaps, especially after last night's storm. Hopefully tomorrow will bring us some more findings," and so George departed for the evening.

Both Dawson and Braxton had worked with George for over three years now and found her easy to work with and very thorough in her job.

George was short for Georgina. The boys could sense she was a bit of a tomboy, with her short hair and manner of calling them chaps. It was quite endearing really. Braxton guessed she was approximately 30 years of age. He had seen her a couple of times at his local bar with her husband, to whom he had previously been introduced.

It was getting late, both Dawson and Braxton decided to reconvene the next day and follow up on the examinations with George at her lab. So the pair of them left for the day. They bid Waites and the rest of the team a good evening, as most of them had reports to finish.

17. Nightmare

There is no room… just a void of total darkness – black. A single ray of light is aimed at what appears to be a long and fat, ugly larva…. sweaty, revolting – repulsive.

It wriggles… but is moving nowhere – stuck. It begins to slowly inflate like a long rippled balloon in slow motion… increasing in its nauseating appearance.

From nowhere… in the top right corner of view – shock. A single bulging eye looks down, amplified by an enormous circular magnifying glass… examining this vile creature.

In one swift single motion, a large hand holding a scalpel inserts a cut deep inside the creature, opening a wound – a surgical slit into the thick skin. In an instant, as the slit is cut, a beam of light screams from out of the fissure – so bright, so blinding. With the intensity of a laser, it hits Braxton full in the eyes. He recoils and screams… "Arrgh… huh?!"

Braxton starts to shake his head from side to side, his hands grasping his bedsheets tight, trying to escape from this nightmare, sweating from the adrenaline of fighting this hideous image. Tina shakes him out of his torment. "Huh?!"

"Braxton! You're having a nightmare! Wake up!" shouts Tina, still shaking him out of his grip and turning on the bedside light.

"Oh, huh, what? Oh that was horrid... I don't want that again!" said Braxton, as his heart pounded with palpitations.

"What was it, Braxton?"

"It was an ugly, vile creature! I think it's about our latest discovery. I've never seen anything like it before in my life! It's not normal, it's almost alien, it's horrid. I have absolutely no idea what it is..." said Braxton in a daze.

"Are you going to be OK? Do you need a drink? I can get you a glass of water, if you like?" asked Tina.

"No... no... thanks, I should be OK. I'll get over it. I just didn't expect it. I'll be all right. Sorry, Tina, it's stupid... really."

After a couple of minutes, and after being reassured that Braxton had returned to a calm state, Tina turned off the light and continued with her slumber.

She couldn't help but wonder what kind of events in Braxton's life, as a Detective Constable, were reducing him to nightmares, for this had not been the first time.

18. Second Examination

The next day, just after lunch, both Dawson and Braxton met with George at the lab to go through the previous day's findings. They were also expecting the results from the other examinations made on the dead couple. George had a good night's sleep, as had most people, mainly due to the previous sleepless night and the storm.

They met George in her office and sat for 10 minutes enjoying afternoon tea and biscuits.

"Did you sleep well, George?" asked Dawson, "I know I did." Braxton was not sure what to say after his nightmare experience.

"Yes, thanks. I went to bed early and was out like a light, in fact as soon as my head hit the pillow. Needed the alarm to wake me up which is a rare thing these days. I wanted my morning coffee, that's for sure!" George spoke with a smile of satisfaction on her face. She took another gulp of her afternoon tea while the men drank theirs.

Having finished their tea, the trio wandered over to the crime lab. "Well chaps…" said George, "I have some more news for you and perhaps I can show you the bodies again – just so that you get the full picture."

George pulled out the two slabs and uncovered the bodies as she continued with her report.

"As you can see they are quite similar in appearance. One is obviously male and the other… well, the bone skeleton structure and DNA suggest she is female. As I said to you last night, she has no internal reproductive organs, and there are no signs of surgery either. So I can only imagine she was like that at birth… very bizarre!

"He's 7ft 7in tall and she is 7ft 9in. How many people do we know of this height? Hopefully your records should be able to pin these two down, Dawson. Have you had any comeback on your identity search?" asked George.

"No, nothing, not yet. But to be honest they do look a little strange. How old would you say they are, George?" asked Dawson.

"Well, this is the thing, Dawson, I'm having the age re-checked, because they came back with unexpected results," replied George.

"What do you mean?" asked Braxton, who was staring at the two bodies as though he seemed to recognise some of their features. It was from a time way back in his youth when he had encountered two old men of similar height in a park. But he quickly shrugged the thought out of his mind.

"Well the results suggest that both of them are around the 110-year mark, but obviously that's an error. We can see that with our own eyes. What would you say they were, Braxton?"

"I'd have them down at 35 or maybe 40. They look in good shape, quite muscular, although tall, perhaps more like a marathon athlete, I'd say," guessed Braxton.

"Exactly! I had them at roughly the same age. We'll get a second set of results tomorrow. But I have to warn you that these type of tests are never 100 per cent accurate," concluded George.

Braxton felt he needed to contribute. "I took the liberty of finding out about seven footers, Sarge. Would you believe there are approximately 2,800 people in the world who are 7ft or taller? Considering the world population is over seven billion people, this means that the percentage of seven footers is extremely rare indeed. In fact they say there are only four people in the world taller than 8ft."

"Thanks, Braxton, that's really helpful," Dawson replied with a hint of sarcasm. "So how many are there in the UK?"

"Don't know, Sarge. Let's hope there aren't many so we can quickly identify these two," replied Braxton.

"Yes, that's the idea, Braxton. Get on to it please, and return to the missing persons as well," requested Dawson as he patted Braxton gently on the shoulder.

"OK, George, then we shall see you tomorrow with more news to help us solve the riddle of the two mummies," Dawson said in an uncharacteristic light hearted way to relieve the tension amongst them. It was clear to all three that this was an unusual case and would set new challenges that none of them had ever faced before.

"Thanks, chaps, I hope to have more information for you. I'll see you to the door," concluded George.

19. Bizarre

The next day brought another dead end – no missing persons over 7ft tall, and George re-confirmed the ages of the couple. The man was 120 years old, the woman was older at 150…. Incredible and beyond comprehension.

Something just didn't add up. Dawson, together with Braxton, started to wonder what the next course of action would be.

"What?! How on earth can they be 120 …. 50… that's just ridiculous, George! You need to go back to your sources and tell them to sort it out! There is no way this couple are that age! All three of us agree they must be in their mid-30s. This is just ridiculous!" ranted Dawson, repeating himself, with both George and Braxton nodding in agreement.

Dawson calmed down slightly, enough to apologise. "Sorry, George. It's just that we don't really have much to go on, and to start with an age that is beyond belief. Isn't the oldest known person in the world somewhere around 120? But a shrivelled old lady at that? … Sorry," Dawson said again apologetically, holding his hands up in acknowledgement of his sharpness.

"That's OK, I understand. I find it hard to believe and still question it myself," George replied calmly and sympathetically.

"OK, let's try something else. What's the cause of death?" asked Dawson.

"Well, the man died of a cardiac arrest, we're very certain about that. It's not uncommon with very tall people, especially of his height, to have this condition, as the heart cannot cope with the demands of a body that size. Other than that he was quite a fit looking man, as you said before, Braxton.

"But as for our lady here, well… I can't find any reason at all, sorry. So far nothing has come up, so I need to do more analysis. Normally this kind of process is quite quick, but we will carry on looking," said George.

Silence followed for a moment as they took it all in, then George went into a little detail about how people reach 7ft. "Apparently it's caused by a condition known as pituitary gigantism, which is the result of an over-production of growth hormones. The growth hormones are released from the pituitary gland in the brain, but if the gland is damaged then it can release too many and so growth is increased."

Braxton had also done his general research as usual and had come up with a number of interesting facts. Referring to his notepad, he said: "I did some more analysis on heights, Sarge. As standards of living and nutrition have improved the average Briton has become three quarters of an inch taller than the previous generation. Official Health of the Nation figures show that 30 per cent of men under 25 are now over 6ft. If the current trend continues then the average British man's height will be 6ft within a couple of generations, and the average woman will be 5ft 7in tall.

"The most bizarre fact concerns the Dutch. The average male height in the Netherlands has risen by 20 cms – that's about eight inches – in the last 150 years, according to military records. By comparison, the height of the average American man has risen a mere six centimetres over the same period. Currently the average height for a man in the Netherlands is over 1.8 metres, just under 6ft. So with a simple extrapolation, in another 150 years they will be on average over two metres tall, that's over six and a half feet, Sarge."

"Wonderful, Braxton, I'm sure it all helps," said Dawson again, not totally impressed with Braxton's trivia.

Dawson was left in a state of frustration. He needed more evidence, more information to go on; two dead bodies, seemingly a couple who have an unusual appearance, lacking any records, no documents or belongings, just turning up from nowhere overnight. They needed a breakthrough, a clue, something….

Dawson decided to assign Braxton to the case. Both Dawson and Braxton were up for promotion soon, and he felt Braxton could do with the responsibility of such an unusual tragedy. At the same time Dawson's frustration at the investigation was also driving him slightly insane through exhaustion, maybe he needed a holiday away from it all.

Dawson took Braxton aside and informed him that he wanted him to take over, and to leave no stone unturned.

20. Dan

Dan was a blond-haired, blue-eyed boy. He had been adopted at the early age of six months by a married couple of men, both of whom were relatively young, but devoted to the upbringing of their new son. There were no brothers or sisters, he was an only child.

Dan had been an artist almost since the moment he could draw breath. His memory was vivid, and he often reminisced about the moments in his childhood where his friends and teachers praised his artistry. At school he won the art prize every year. Typically, he would win a digital art book or, as was the fashion, a real quality hard-back publication – a rarity and piece of art in its own right.

He often dreamed that one day he would be able to publish a book with his own art, an ambition from an early age. He had plenty of time on his side to develop his skills and, who knows, he might one day exhibit in galleries near and far. There was a certain romance in the ideal of dedicating his life to the world of art.

Dan adored the Renaissance period between the 14th and 17th centuries, including of course the magnificent Leonardo da Vinci, Michelangelo, and Raphael. Dan loved the concept of a rebirth ideology. For someone of such a tender age, he intuitively comprehended that people of a certain maturity often desired a change in their life's direction. He had read up about this, and had heard about something called a mid-life crisis, where certain individuals craved an alternate life style – a re-birth... a renaissance.

Dan's love of traditional art meant that he hadn't cared too much for abstract or contemporary art. He felt it was for those who technically couldn't draw or paint. To slap some paint onto a canvas, then examine it in order to determine the title or theme after the painting was completed, was not art – it was just an interpretation of a mess. Most paintings like this were typically called Atmosphere or Opus.

Dan knew that art needed a new style to inject fresh interest from enthusiasts, under the guise of opening up their spirit and expressionism. What better way to introduce the art world to enthusiasts lacking artistic ability? So more and more themes and ideologies were developed. But these new modern movements were not for Dan. He would perhaps accept the Impressionists, and at times the Cubists, but that was it. This was of course Dan's own interpretation of art. He recognised that this appreciation of art was the beauty in the eye of the beholder – as was all art.

He was an intelligent young man and perhaps he should have developed his study of psychology, but he preferred to delve into symbolism and geometry in his compositions. He had an incredible sense of imagination, almost intuition. He could always be found doodling, formulating new ideas and designs from a very early age.

One of his fathers demonstrated some drawing ability. Perhaps it was this that piqued Dan's interest in the world of art. He had even kept an earlier drawing sketched by his father when they were on holiday together in Cornwall during his childhood.

Dan's earliest memory was venturing to school with his fathers in the freezing snow, heavy winds slammed shut the garden gate and snow built up on the metal wire fence. There were snowball fights as well as the traditional building of snowmen together. They would return home to a log fire and stand in front of the roaring flames until their fingers ached with chilblains and the back of their legs slowly cooked.

Dan never realised that having two fathers was anything other than normal, in these times it was the norm for same sex parentage. He hadn't missed out on having a mother, although at times he wondered what it would be like to have a sibling.

At school he bonded well with his art teacher. Art was his preferred subject and Ms Barnes was his favourite teacher. Without realising it, by adopting a woman confidante Dan had found a way to establish the need for an older female influence in his life.

Ms Barnes was in effect his replacement mother. It was only through her he felt he could show his softer, more artistic side. This would be no different for children who had two mothers. They too, without realising it, would adopt a male teacher or uncle to confide in. It's funny how human nature finds a way to balance the equation.

The other love of Dan's life was sport, in particular he loved to kick a football about from the earliest of ages, from the moment he could stand on his two feet.

There were even old movies of Dan at the tender age of two kicking a ball. Another clip demonstrated him running and aiming to kick the ball, but completely missing and falling on his face. The ball almost appeared to be half his height. It was so cute and amusing.

With his sport and art, Dan's mind was so fully occupied that he had not really been aware of boys or girls. In essence, he was a late developer in his adolescence. He wasn't aware that people were supposed to be homosexual or heterosexual. What's that all about?

But as he grew older he became aware of the trend in society which moved from a heterosexual to a homosexual orientation. He felt no inclination towards homosexuality or heterosexuality and didn't even think about it. Instead he focused on his sport and art. In fact, without even realising it his ignorance was his escapism and perhaps his innocence. For Dan had just not yet reached this stage of his life.

21. Mich

Mich's earliest recollection as a child came from an emotion. Something locked up, deep inside. It was one of rejection, one of isolation, but she couldn't explain it. There were no images that came with this emotion. It was a mystery to Mich and left her with an emptiness inside.

By contrast, one of her earliest memories was of the hours spent playing in the playground of a local park. She loved the slides and roundabouts, hopping around enjoying a game of hopscotch and skipping. This conjured up memories of fun, happiness, love and joy.

At this young age Mich was such a tactile person. She was always wanting to hug and kiss the cheeks of friends and family, for she was a very affectionate child, wanting to say hello to anyone who passed by. Mich's world was a happy world.

Some children are blessed more than others, and it soon became evident that Mich was bright and very intelligent. Her ability to learn quickly did not go unnoticed by her father who encouraged her as much as he could. She learned to play the piano and the guitar, to memorise facts and historical events and to pick up new languages.

As a young child she made friends easily. But it's usually not until the early teens that children can be cruel. Mich had been born with alopecia - a condition which leaves the body with no hair. For a time, this caused her some grief with bullying and name calling at her school.

Fortunately, the bullying came to an end. Thanks to the world of fashion Mich found herself to be a trendsetter as famous models and movie stars started sporting bald looks. As a result, Mich was seen as an attractive, fashionable young lady. In fact, in this homosexually dominated society it was the girls who found her more appealing.

As Mich grew older she developed into a beautiful, tall young-woman. She had shot up in height during her teen years. Her clean look, bald head and height meant she received no end of requests for modelling from an early age. She had become a fashionable commodity.

However, Mich found this popularity curious, since she valued her intelligence more than her looks. She preferred a good old book rather than a fashion show. Her knowledge meant more to her than the attention of her admirers. She wanted to go to university and study. It was with this in mind that Mich continued to further her education, studying palaeoanthropology, anthropogeny and anthropology.

22. Dan and Mich

There was one characteristic of Mich that was, without question, slightly humorous and endearing. She was rather clumsy. Many a time she would knock drinks over, bump into people, forget to bring something important to a meeting... and so it goes on. Her father once said she would forget her head one day. Perhaps it was because her mind was so full of everything she was learning.

Mich first met Dan at a coming out party. In fact she bumped into him, and with her elbow knocked a drink completely out of his hand and onto the floor. As she turned to apologise, she noticed a look of shock on Dan's face, with his gaping jaw and eyes pursuing the can of beer as it flew skyward across the room. He hadn't even noticed Mich as he tried to rescue his beverage.

Mich was very apologetic, but Dan was already motoring towards the table where the excess of drinks were stocked. For some reason, Mich followed him. She wanted to ensure her apology was accepted.

"Oh, sorry! Did you say something?" Dan commented to Mich over the noise of the music, cupping his hand to his ear to hear better.

"Yes, I said that I'm sorry!" shouted Mich, wanting to be heard above the noise.

"Sorry? What for?" asked Dan with a puzzled look.

"I knocked your drink out of your hand."

"Oh, sorry. I hadn't realised you were apologising. I didn't hear you. I'm really sorry! It's quite loud in here, isn't it?" said Dan.

"You don't have to apologise. It's me who should be apologising to you!"

"Yes, of course, sorry! Well, apology accepted! No harm done, eh?"

"Do you always apologise when you haven't done anything wrong?" asked Mich.

"You know… I've never really thought about it. …. Sorry," and so they both burst out laughing.

Mich found herself wanting to stay with Dan and chat some more. "Well I'm Mich, pleased to meet you." She offered her hand in a lady-like fashion and they shook hands quite formally in a joking manner.

"Likewise. I'm Dan. Nice to have bumped in to you," and again they both laughed.

They chatted through the evening, relaying their accounts on how they knew the host, which college they were attending, where they were resident on campus, and what they were studying. They realised that their studies were in completely different fields, but at the same time they found each other's subject fascinating. After a while, they realised that they missed these subjects in their lives.

"You know, Mich, you have an interesting head. Maybe you would let me draw it?"

"You mean do my portrait?"

"No, no. I mean etch the contours of your head. It's such a lovely and curious shape," qualified Dan.

"Well, that's a new one for me, Dan. I've heard of seeing your etchings, or drawing my body, but to draw the contour of my cranium wins the prize!" Again, they burst out laughing.

As the evening progressed both Dan and Mich had forgotten that the room was full of people, of friends and acquaintances, they were so wrapped up in their flow of conversation.

They exchanged numbers and became friends on social media without hesitation – something neither of them would normally do. It just seemed right. They agreed to meet at the local café the next day, close to the university campus.

The café would become a regular meeting place for the two of them, whether starting the day with a coffee and breakfast, a quick bite at lunch time, or a beer before meeting up later for movies and parties. They even had a regular table, where they would sit and survey passers-by through the window on the street outside.

23. The Beginning of Civilisation 5000 and 3500 BC

Joe had his college friend Glyn visiting one evening for a few beers. They were overdue a get together. While most young men would talk about sport, both Joe and Glyn were more into their conspiracy theories, or perhaps that should say Joe's conspiracy theories.

"I tell you, Glyn, most, if not all of our old history books are now full of untruths, a fact in itself, simply because new discoveries are always being made and sometimes they contradict existing facts. History is completely full of incorrect theories – some were fundamentally way off the mark! Remember the flat Earth theory and how the Sun had circled our planet?" declared Joe.

"Ah, well, I think the Flat Earth Society will have something to say about that. The flat Earth theory is coming back, Joe!" quipped Glyn with a slight grin.

"Bonkers, the lot of them," said Joe. "But it's true that if new discoveries change the course of our history, then ergo that means it's very possible that what we read today may also be proven untrue in the future. The writers would have to state that the fact was known at a certain point in time, rather than state it as an absolute truth."

"Here's another example, Glyn – take dinosaurs. Dinosaurs lived apart from humans in another millennia. But then they discovered that early Man and late dinosaur walked the planet at the same time. History re-written!"

"At one time the number of planets in our planetary system was nine. Pluto became de-classified... then reclassified. Now there is currently a search for another rogue planet that seems to be within an orbit so far away it only comes close to Earth every 3000 years, motioning in the opposite direction to the others ... apparently!"

"The real big news of today is our revised view of the planets, the universe and beyond. In the past, it was unknown how many planets existed in our galaxy or universe, if any existed at all. But now, new planets are being discovered throughout, some that may be potentially similar to our Earth. They're called geo-planets. As far as we know, there are many hundreds and eventually there may be thousands – where was that written?" continued Joe.

"It just gets better, Glyn! Revelations are being made all the time! Who would have thought that over a hundred years ago, people would encounter anti-matter, black holes and dark matter, the Boson particle and even the Big Bang were all unknown."

"These new discoveries didn't mean that they didn't exist before. It's mind boggling to even wonder about the entities we don't know yet. Perhaps there is something that would revolutionise our entire way of life even today. Wouldn't that be awesome, Glyn?!" Joe was on a roll, for he loved this whole spectrum of revelations.

"Remember how electricity was detected? It's not man-made, it's an actual physical property that exists. One only has to find further revelations that use electricity and so the momentum of further discoveries and inventions continues.

"Where would we be without electricity? No computers, no television, no internet, no virtual reality and so it goes on. Could there be something we don't know about today that will eventually replace electricity?" quizzed Joe.

"Well, that's very true, Joe, where would we be without computers, mobile phones and mp3 players? More sociable, probably! Maybe we would talk to people face to face and not through a screen. Don't get me wrong, I agree it's an advancement in one way, but sometimes I do wonder where all this technology will lead to. There is so much more information at our fingertips, but I think sometimes it comes at a cost of losing touch with reality," said Glyn, with his philosophical outlook on life.

"I see what you mean," reflected Joe. "But, anyway, that's not what I was talking about. I'm on about the fact that our history books are continually being re-written. And so what I was trying to say was that when it comes to our earliest civilisations here on

Earth, new discoveries imply that our ancient civilisation may go back further than we think. Is history about to be rewritten again?"

"Well, Joe, it sounds like you think it is!" They laughed and supped their beers.

"Glyn, I've been looking at the latest information about the pyramids. If the ones of Egypt were an example, then history said the sphinx was built in approximately 2500 BC. But when it was discovered that the surrounding banks were eroded by floods, it became apparent that the sphinx was possibly built over 12,000 years ago, or even further back than that. The precise alignment of the three large pyramids with the Orion constellation was also approximately 12,000 years ago. There's even a theory that the sphinx goes back to 800,000 years ago! This really opens up the argument for the history books to be rewritten," said Joe.

"I also found out that one of the very first civilisations known to us in our history books is the Mesopotamians, in a region situated within the Tigris-Euphrates river system. In modern times this is roughly most of Iraq, Kuwait, eastern parts of Syria, south east of Turkey and along the borders between Turkey and Syria as well as Iran. It's such a shame that there is so much war in the area. If only they could live in peace and appreciate what they have, their history and architecture to marvel at.

"The region called Mesopotamia provided some of the earliest cities in world history that appeared between 5000 and

3500 BC by the Sumerian people," Joe added. "If these were the people regarded as the first, then which civilisation would have the genius to build such pyramids 5000 years before them, or the sphinx at an impossible age of 800,000 years ago?"

"I've no idea, Joe! But, my beer's nearly finished."

24. Civilisations around 10,000 BC

"OK, Joe… if, as you say, the sphinx and potentially some of the pyramids were constructed more than 12,000 years ago, then who were the civilisations that existed around this time? Tell me!" said Glyn.

Joe thought it best to look this one up on the internet in response to Glyn's question. "OK, Glyn, give me a sec and we'll see."

Joe pulled up a website showing information relevant to the topic and started to paraphrase an article to Glyn. "Well, as an example, *the region of Mesopotamia is the site of the earliest developments of the Neolithic Revolution from around 10,000 BC. It was identified as having inspired some of the most important developments in human history including the invention of the wheel, the planting of the first cereal crops and the development of handwriting, mathematics, astronomy and agriculture.* But again, as I keep saying, this is only conjecture or a theory by academics. I mean, I find it hard to believe the wheel was only invented then as it just seems a natural shape to invent, doesn't it?" said Joe.

"*The city of Jericho in the Palestinian Territories and near the Jordan River in the West Bank is believed to be one of the oldest inhabited cities in the world. It was thought to have the oldest stone tower in the world, but excavations at Tell Qaramel in Syria have discovered some even older.*

"Archaeologists have unearthed the remains of more than 20 successive settlements in Jericho, the first of which dates back 11,000 years (9000 BC), almost to the very beginning of the Holocene Epoch of the Earth's history. The Holocene Epoch is the current period of geologic time, sometimes referred to as the Anthropocene Epoch, although a group of geologists, climate scientists and ecologists consider the Anthropocene Epoch to be the current Epoch and consider the Holocene Epoch finished," quoted Joe.

"But the definition of the Holocene Epoch is not entirely true as modern humans were already well established long before the epoch began. The Holocene Epoch began 11,500 to 12,000 years ago at the close of the Palaeolithic Ice Age and continues through today," continued Joe.

"The Palaeolithic Epoch is also known as the Old Stone Age."

"Ahhh! Ok! I see, just like the Flintstones!" grinned Glyn.

"It was a period in which humans grouped together in small societies such as bands and lived their lives by gathering plants, fishing, hunting or scavenging wild animals. Their tools were crude using stone, wood or bone - they even used leather and plant fibres.

"*During the end of the Palaeolithic Epoch humans began to produce the earliest works of art and engage in religious and spiritual behaviour such as burials and rituals. As far back as 50,000 years ago academics started to see a more enriched set of artefacts including such items as projectile points, engraving tools, knife blades, drilling and piercing tools.*" Joe finished reading the article.

"OK, so what do you think? Could these people, who lived with such basic tools and equipment, be capable of constructing ancient pyramids of such precision? A precision that would be difficult even with today's standards of industrial equipment?" Joe looked Glyn straight in the eye.

"Nope! Never!" Glyn replied. "It's hard to believe, isn't it? I think I'll have one more beer and then call it a night," and so Glyn went off to grab two more beers from the fridge.

25. Transition

Richard Braxton was a young 28-year-old, slim, an average 5ft 8in tall, with short ginger hair. He was a bright, intelligent man, studied and worked hard to accomplish his position of Detective Constable in the CID.

His energy and affinity with solving mysteries, together with his ability to retain useless trivia, was an asset – even if it did wind up Detective Sergeant Dawson on the odd occasion.

At times his job could become very stressful, to the point where on rare occasions it would cause him to suffer nightmares. Braxton also knew that he needed time to detach himself from his occupation, a time to relax and chill. One of his favourite ways to unwind from work was to spend time with friends and family. So on most Wednesday evenings he could be found at the local bar, The Dog and Duck. The bar was one of the most popular fashionable watering holes, conveniently only a 15-minute walk away from Braxton and Tina's home. They met up every Wednesday for the ever-popular quiz night.

The quiz night involved several teams of four, invariably with friends or family. Braxton had formed his team with a married couple, Gerry and Sally, who he had known since his school days. The fourth member of the team was Tina, his girlfriend of three years.

Typically, each team would have a silly name. After much thought, Braxton, Tina, Gerry and Sally called themselves the BLTs. Rather than a bacon, lettuce and tomato sandwich the team's name was actually taken from their surnames - Braxton, Gerry and Sally Liston, and Tina Thomas. The name was short and simple, and in fact they often ate BLTs at the bar with their drinks. At one point they had thought about the name BLT & G&T, but settled for BLT as they mostly drank beer.

Braxton's younger brother Joe was also the BLTs' substitute member. This arrangement suited Joe. As a poor student he knew the team would treat him all evening with snacks and supply him with as much beer as he could drink.

Braxton would prepare for the quiz throughout the week by keeping up to date with current affairs, reading general history and literature. He would also keep on top of any research required as part of a recent crime case. He was always researching.

As a child, Braxton was a bookworm, often reading his parents' books or spending hours at the local library. He would soak up every documentary on the television or internet. His brain was a sponge for knowledge.

He would spend many hours with Tina discussing the rights and wrongs of the world. Both would ensure their arguments were well supported with facts and evidence, to the point where Braxton had often thought that Tina should have joined the police force as she was quite thorough in her research and debates.

Tina's forte had been history from ancient to modern times, having studied it at university. Although an avid reader of novels, she also read non-fiction - biographical or historical.

Tina was a little vertically challenged at 5ft tall and sometimes she would compensate by wearing high-heeled shoes, although she hated stilettoes. She had been a tomboy in her younger years and had even worn Dr Martens in her goth years. She previously would have dyed her blonde hair a bright pink or purple or even luminous green, but since she met Braxton she had returned to her natural blonde as if content with her life.

Her other forte was music, mainly from listening rather than playing an instrument. She enjoyed such a varied selection of favourite music that spanned the spectrum, from classical to goth, to rock. She even tried to keep up with the charts – knowing they usually came up in the pub quiz. Braxton and Tina would share their musical tastes during their evenings together, where their common ground was rock and classical music – although Braxton also had a soft spot for jazz.

Having already just completed some research on the increase of human height around the world, Braxton now knew that the Netherlands was the tallest nation, especially after their rapid growth over the last century and a half.

He couldn't help but wonder what other changes had occurred over recent centuries.

But tonight the main theme of the evening's discussion, especially for his team, was over the LGBT. It only takes one question in the quiz to spark a heavy discussion within and across the teams, and this could often overflow into the rest of the week through emails and messaging on social media.

Certainly one of the big changes occurring at the moment was the rise of the LGBT movement. Questions relating to this subject often arose in the quiz night.

"What does LGBT stand for?"

"Answer: Lesbian Gay Bi Trans-sexual."

"What decade was the LGBT movement created?" They had had no idea, but they were soon to find out.

"Answer: 1980s." The answer caused a considerable volume of noise in the bar, as they all contested this date, citing that different movements with the same ideals had been founded throughout history.

"What are the colours of the LGBT Pride flag?"

"Answer: Every bloody colour going," remarked one of the team. It hadn't been far from the truth. "One could say all the colours of the rainbow." This often resulted in a heated discussion amongst the BLTs, who were slightly biased, and other teams sitting close by, all being heterosexual and with perhaps slightly bigoted views.

"I wouldn't mind but they've taken all the decent colours and so there's nothing left for heterosexuals to create their own flag. I read somewhere that a flag had been proposed for heterosexuals. Do you know what so called colours they were proposing? I'll tell you! There were going to be five horizontal colours – starting from the top with jet black, next a slightly duller black then a very dark grey, followed by a medium grey and ending at the bottom with a light grey!"

"I think there is something wrong here – don't you? Perhaps it's just best we wave our white flags," ranted someone from another team listening in on the conversation.

"Hmm," Braxton could feel they had touched a nerve there.

It became apparent to his team members that swotting up on the subject of LGBT would guarantee a point most weeks. One of the team, Gerry, had suggested that the quizmaster was in fact been a member of the LGBT, and was trying to promote the movement to his audience. As if the quizmaster really needed to do so – the LGBT had already become very fashionable and trendy.

"Well, it has become fashionable! Only recently we were in Copenhagen prior to the Gay Pride Parade, and most cars and all the buses were driving through the city with Gay Pride flags waving at each side weeks before and after the event. The same colours were painted on the sides of walls, on shop windows, out of apartments – the whole city had been taken over by the LGBT colours.

"You could see the attraction of it, because it was promoting peace, happiness, joy and colour. The whole event attracted almost everyone including heterosexuals who thought that, yes… it's trendy…. almost hippie in one way.

"It was so positive. But why is that just for LGBT, why did it take the LGBT community to do this?"

There followed a brief pause of silence amongst the team members who were not quite sure what the answer could be.

On the table next to the BLTs was a team of four – two couples of a similar age to Braxton. They kept looking over to the BLTs as if interested in the topic under discussion. Braxton had often noticed this team in the bar and especially at quiz night, so he felt obliged to introduce himself and his team.

As with any introduction on the bar's quiz night, it started with team names, so Braxton kicked off with "Hi, we're the BLTs, I'm Braxton…. this is Tina, my girlfriend, and friends from my schooldays, Gerry and Sally Liston."

"Hi, nice to meet you, we're the LGBTs……

"I'm Seb. This is Chaz, short for Charlie, my husband. This is Brenda and her wife Tracey, we couldn't help but notice that you were complimenting Gay Pride. It's amazing, isn't it? When you think how far the LGBT movement has come, don't you think?"

"Absolutely…." Braxton spontaneously replied. "Oh, my! So they really are two couples, but not what I was expecting. This is the sign of the times," he thought.

Braxton and Tina left Gerry and Sally to continue the rest of the evening in the company of the LGBTs. Braxton had to be in the office early and Tina was eager for a loving cuddle.

The following evening, Braxton's phone rang and on the other end of the line was Gerry. After some idle chit-chat, Gerry asked Braxton and Tina to dinner at his place on the Friday. Gerry then went on to explain that just after Braxton and Tina had left the pub, he had also invited the LGBTs – who had excitedly agreed to come. They thought it could make for an interesting and thought provoking evening.

Braxton graciously accepted the invite on behalf of himself and Tina. He also acknowledged that the event should be entertaining, as he thanked Gerry and Sally. He decided to do some research on the LGBT phenomenon in preparation of the event.

26. Our Anthropocene Epoch

"So, Glyn, do you know what epoch we are currently in?" asked Joe as he supped his third beer.

"Nope! No idea. But I get the impression you're about to tell me, aren't you?" suggested Glyn with a slight grin on his face.

"I am indeed. We are now in the Anthropocene Epoch which is named because its primary characteristic is the global changes caused by human activity," explained Joe.

"It's a very significant epoch for many reasons, Glyn! Because pressure from the human population has had far-reaching effects on the biodiversity of the planet. Earth has undergone at least five major mass extinction events, events that have killed more than 60 per cent of all living bodies on the planet. The last mass extinction closed the Cretaceous Period 65 million years ago and resulted in the extinction of the dinosaurs," said Joe.

"So why is it significant?" asked Joe rhetorically. "Because many scientists believe we are now in the midst of a sixth mass extinction event caused by Man!

"Based on population numbers required to maintain genetic viability it is estimated that as many as 30 per cent of plant and animal species may become extinct within the next 100 years, with habitat destruction the leading cause of the extinction of many species today.

"Since the beginning of the 21st Century alone a number of animals and plants have become extinct. Here… let me show you the list of animals as an example to illustrate this sad set of events …." suggested Joe. He pulled the list up on his laptop and read it out to Glyn. The name of each species was met with a sadness, realising that these animals will never be seen again.

In 2011 the eastern cougar that once lived in north eastern North America was declared extinct by the U.S. Fish and Wildlife Service with the last known individual trapped and killed by Man in 1938.

The western black rhinoceros or West African black rhinoceros is a subspecies of the black rhinoceros. In 2011 it was declared extinct by the International Union for Conservation of Nature (IUCN). It was once widespread in the savanna of sub-Saharan Africa and resided primarily in Cameroon, but its numbers declined due to poaching.

Also in 2011 the Japanese river otter was declared extinct by the country's Ministry of the Environment, after not being seen for more than 30 years.

In 2012 the last known Pinta Island tortoise died. It was a species of the Galapagos tortoise and had been native to the Ecuador Pinta Island. It was thought to have been wiped out by Man and his hunting.

In 2013 the Formosan clouded leopard of Taiwan was officially declared extinct, it had such a beautiful pattern of markings on its fur. Gone forever.

In 2014 the Bermuda saw-whet owl was declared extinct. It is not known what caused its extinction, but it may have been related to the decline of cedar and palmetto trees, or the arrival of non-native predators and competitors after human colonisation.

In 2016 the Bramble Cay melomys, a cute little rodent, was declared extinct. Also known as the Bramble Cay mosaic-tailed rat, it was from the rodent family that was prominent in herd-fields and strandline vegetation where it built burrows. It was one of Australia's most isolated mammals living in Bramble Cay just off Queensland at the northern end of the Great Barrier Reef.

"That was only part of a huge list. I tell you, Glyn, the sad aspect of this catastrophe is that it will continue to grow in the future! Why? Because history has told us this happens all the time during the course of our evolution, and Man is not helping the situation," conceded Joe.

"Already now, there is another list of other animals that are close to extinction. We joke about the demise of the comical dodo bird, but this is a very serious issue that needs to be addressed by Man, as it is Man that seems to be one of the major causes of such atrocities! Sometimes I feel ashamed of our race." Joe had hit a solemn moment.

"Animals such as the incredibly beautiful cheetah could soon be gone. Their skin and meat is prized by poachers, while cubs are targeted by traffickers to sell as status symbols in the Middle East.

"Let me check the internet to see what else is endangered....

"Oh no! Just listen to this list... The African elephant is vulnerable, the Asian elephant is endangered, the Bengal tiger – endangered, blue whale – endangered, the bonobo and the chimpanzee are endangered, oh heck ... the black rhino, Bornean orangutan and cross river gorilla are all 'critically endangered'... I just don't believe this, I can't read it anymore. I'm speechless!

"Reminds me of the phrase 'forever and for ever', as in – gone in time and gone beyond time, forever in eternity. Could it get any worse Glyn?"

"Sounds to me like Man needs to understand the greater threat to our environment and our evolution," agreed Glyn.

"Do you know what's even scarier, Glyn? When the gene pool withers to nothing – then the species dies and becomes extinct!

"Is this about to happen to Man?

"Is there to be a '*devolution*'?"

27. Making a Baby

Gerry and Sally had invited Braxton and Tina round to their home for an evening meal. As was customary, Braxton and Tina arrived with a bottle of red wine for the man and a small bouquet of flowers for the lady.

Braxton and Tina lived just around the corner from Gerry and Sally, so they decided to take a pleasant evening stroll. The rain had dispersed and left the air fresh and clean – perfect for a totally invigorating walk. Wearing their heavy coats and with cold, deep breaths filling their lungs, Braxton and Tina walked hand in hand and talked about how the evening might unfold.

They arrived on time, completely refreshed and ready to be entertained. Big hugs were exchanged between the two couples, and the guests' coats were left hanging on the end of the bannister as they were shown into the cosy lounge.

The house had an identical layout to Braxton and Tina's, so it was almost home from home. Gerry and Sally seemed to go for a more cluttered look, with little knick-knacks everywhere and lots of dark colours. In contrast, Braxton and Tina preferred a more minimalist look with very little furniture and colour.

In the lounge they were greeted by another couple sitting in front of the fire. It was Brenda and her wife Tracey from the LGBT quiz night team. Braxton recognised the pair – Brenda had short, cropped, almost punk dark hair and was wearing jeans. In contrast Tracey had a softer look with mousy, bobbed hair and wore a dress. Both were about the same size, around 5ft 3in, taller than Tina – but then most people were. Brenda did most of the talking. Tracey seemed to prefer it this way, as she sat in the background listening in on the chat.

Sally mentioned that Seb and Chaz couldn't make it to the get together as they had had a row over adoption. Braxton and Tina looked at each other, but neither said anything. Instead, they swiftly moved on to another topic.

The wine flowed as all six of them sat for a while discussing the latest news and events of the week. Wars were being fought, politicians battled in hustings and sports teams were competing in stadiums across the world. An interesting analogy ensued where they each realised that no matter the size of the region being discussed, there was always some conflict within a local town or village, even between neighbours. Finally, they came to the conclusion that this had been human nature from the beginning of time and it wasn't likely to change now.

While discussing battles between villages, Brenda revealed that she played for the local village ladies' football team as an attacking right winger. Apparently she had been an excellent sprinter in her school days and her speed was an asset. She and her team were doing well – they were second in the local ladies' league. They were due a match on Sunday and were playing at the same venue where the quiz night was held.

Braxton, Tina, Gerry and Sally were invited to pop down and give a cheer to Brenda's team, as both couples admitted that neither of them had ever witnessed a ladies' football match. All agreed that it sounded like good fun and that they would go to the game, meeting beforehand for lunch in the bar.

The subject of Seb and Chaz arose again. It seemed that Seb had wanted a baby through adoption and that Chaz wasn't ready to start a family yet. This all felt strange to Braxton, as he couldn't get his head around the concept of a child having two fathers and no mother.

Surely there must be a mother in this process – so how did that work? Wouldn't the child miss out on certain motherly ways? Was that important? Tina could see that Braxton was itching to debate this but signalled to him to wait until he returned home to discuss it with her. She looked at him as if to say: "Leave it, let's discuss it later," using their mutual telepathy.

Both Braxton and Tina knew that their time for starting a family would come later. In their early phase they still enjoyed their relationship. They felt they were still quite young and wanted to travel and explore the world together first. They also agreed between them that pets could come later too, for now they didn't want any ties holding them down. One night as they chatted in bed they did have a laugh at the thought of having a baby with a carrot top coloured hair running riot around the house. They expected he or she would be a wild child with a hot temper, as most redheads' reputations go.

It wasn't long before Gerry and Sally admitted to the group that they too had been trying for over two years to conceive a baby but were struggling. They had consulted the doctor on a multitude of visits and from the many examinations it seemed that Gerry had a low sperm count – practically zero, as the doctor had sensitively phrased it. The doctor put it down to Gerry's previous years of heavy smoking, especially cannabis, or weed as it was often called. Gerry had quit all his vices for quite a while now as he realised his health would suffer. Not only that, but Sally had been strong enough to bully him out of it.

Gerry and Sally were finally recommended for IVF, an abbreviation for in vitro fertilisation, a procedure that would give them a better chance of conception. Their first appointment was planned for the following week and together they were very excited at the prospect, giving them new hope for their dream.

Even Brenda and Tracey admitted that they were content for the moment, enjoying their romantic courtship. But they admitted their time would come. They wanted Tracey to have a baby with a semen donor. Brenda would play the role of the father with Tracey as the mother, because Tracey had always wanted to be a mother.

Braxton decided to research IVF. He wanted to know why so many people seemed to be using the treatment now more than ever.

28. Procreation by Science

Braxton delved into the internet, his regular source of information, to research IVF. It seems that it has only been since the 20th Century that science has helped those who struggle with conception.

It only needs one person in a heterosexual relationship to have a problem for years to pass by without a child, before couples seek advice and either turn to science or adoption.

In the case of homosexual relationships, it is obvious that a surrogate is necessary, and in the majority of cases this also requires an artificial process for the insemination.

Homeopathic remedies were available before science. They were and are still used for those who are anti-science, or where they believe their God will do his will. Truth be told, the remedies are only able to improve the chances alongside a healthier diet and exercise – so no miracles there.

One of the first science-based aids was artificial insemination, in which sperm was placed in the uterus for conception to happen normally. It was in effect a very basic procedure with a low success rate.

However to improve the chances of conception IVF, was introduced – one of several techniques available that produced what were at the beginning known as test-tube babies.

Louise Brown, born in England in 1978, was the first such baby to be conceived outside of her mother's womb. Her parents had received 'menacing' and 'scary' mail in the months after her ground-breaking birth which attracted controversy. Religious leaders expressed concerns about the use of artificial intervention, with some raising fears that science was creating Frankenbabies.

Her family had received post-bags full of mail, including one package containing letters covered in red liquid, a broken glass test tube and a plastic foetus, accompanied by menacing notes.

During the IVF treatment an egg is removed from the woman's ovaries and fertilised with sperm in a laboratory. The fertilised egg, called an embryo, is then returned to the woman's womb to grow and develop naturally.

It can be carried out using the couple's own eggs and sperm, or with eggs and/or sperm from donors.

IVF involves six main stages:

1. Suppressing the natural menstrual cycle with medication
2. Boosting the egg supply with medication to encourage the ovaries to produce more eggs than usual
3. Monitoring the progress and maturing the eggs using an ultrasound scan, with medication to help them mature

4. Collecting the eggs by inserting a needle into the ovaries, via the vagina

5. Fertilising the eggs by mixing them with the sperm for a few days

6. Transferring one or two fertilised eggs (embryos) into the womb

Once the embryo is transferred into the womb, there is a two-week wait to see if the treatment has worked.

In 2010, the percentage of IVF treatments that resulted in a live birth was:

- 32.2% for women under 35

- 27.7% for women aged 35-37

- 20.8% for women aged 38-39

- 13.6% for women aged 40-42

- 5% for women aged 43-44

- 1.9% for women aged over 44

Braxton concluded that IVF wasn't very romantic. It was done in a laboratory with chemicals for medication. It didn't always result in pregnancy and it could be both physically and emotionally demanding.

But there were thought to be close to six million IVF babies across the world as of the early 21st Century, and as each year passed thousands more couples would use the treatment.

29. Early View of Family Life

How far back in time are we able to understand the roles within family life?

It was known that families in the Stone Age were tribal. Individual families would remain close together with the young protecting the elders. The role of the men, the fathers, would be to hunt for meat. The women, along with the children, would forage for seeds, nuts, fruit, vegetables and eggs. The latter was almost a guaranteed certainty, whilst the hunting could be unpredictable and often fruitless.

Perhaps one will never know about the history of relationships between men and women. Was there such a concept of husband and wife during these times? Nor will we ever know about homosexual or asexual relationships from the distant past.

Scholars today have now stated that life in Stone Age times did not consist of the typical husband and wife relationship that was previously regarded as the norm. Families were in fact part of a commune. In this community, at any given time a woman could have sexual or romantic relations with several men or women. Similarly, men could have relations with a number of women, or even men, either all at the same time, or one after the other. But these relationships between several partners were with known people within the commune, and not necessarily with outside strangers. There was no concept of marriage for life. Scholars believe that the role of the father was shared within the commune, in such a way that a child would therefore have many fathers and even many mothers in the sense of guardians.

If one looks into more recent times, such as the Victorian period, the husband was usually a working man, whilst his wife stayed at home and possibly educated the children. The middle to upper classes would most likely have had servants with cooking and cleaning duties.

The term 'nuclear family' gave rise to the typical scenario of husband and wife living together with their children up to the 20th Century.

But the late 20th Century to the 22nd Century saw a number of changes, and one of the most significant was in family life.

Heterosexual relationships generally formed the basis of communities in the 20th Century. The husband was the head of the house, the man who brought the money into the household, while the wife would stay at home to look after the children and make the house a home.

The classic 1950s home economics book *Tips to look after your husband* caused a stir in society. Some people reacted with shock while others reacted with amusement.

Aimed at women, it offered a series of guidelines on how to be the perfect wife. From preparing 'a delicious meal on time' to wearing ribbons in their hair and ensuring they were 'fresh looking', and from going through the house ensuring it was clean and tidy just before the husband returned home from a day's work, to ensuring the home was free from the noise of household appliances and children. It claimed to be everything every dutiful wife needed to know.

Modern Man came about towards the end of the 20th Century. In retrospect 1950s couples, as described in the book, would seem rather archaic, quite ridiculous and almost laughable. Had it not been for the fact that this was truthfully published, one would not believe domestic lifestyles had ever been this way.

30. Modern View of Family Life

Slowly at first, more demands were put on modern day couples to meet financial obligations. Consequently, women also needed an income to supplement their husband's salary. This continued for a number of years until women realised their need for independence, not just to supplement the household income, but to advance their own careers.

This created unease in society. Older men especially felt the growing number of working women was causing high levels of unemployment among men. Women should stay at home the same as always – in any case there was nothing derogatory about being a housewife, the men would say.

The man had not just been the breadwinner in those early days, he had been a company owner, power maker and leading figure in all walks of life, while the woman was the strength behind him. But soon the women would step out from behind the men and become leading figures in their own right, especially over the course of the late 20th Century and through the 21st Century.

The woman's new strength and independence also saw more openness in her desire to be with her own kind – her own sex. At the same time the man was slowly losing strength and would seek passion with his own sex. In short the social demography was rapidly diversifying.

Families were broken up with couples divorcing more and more. Children found themselves with more than one mother and father figures through further marriages or partnerships. Heterosexual marriages would break up while homosexual marriages were legalised. The result was a huge upsurge in adoptions that would see children with two mothers or two fathers.

There was also an increase in the number of friend-families. Those who could not have children sought close relationships with friends who they saw as their surrogate families. Birthdays and festive activities were shared with friend-families; it seemed to fill a gap in a person's life. Most typically with this type of family pets replaced the role of children. Pets that were doted upon, mollycoddled and pampered. Pets that wore woolly hats or jackets knitted by their 'parents'. Pets that had Christmas presents to unwrap with their bare teeth. Pets that had reserved places or seats in the home.

Dan was adopted as a baby by two fathers, whereas Mich's father was a single parent.

One-parent families also became more common, with single people either adopting or having a child through an anonymous donor. Mich did not know her surrogate mother, her father never discussed the subject. A surrogate for a single parent was a subject not discussed nor disclosed, for the surrogate's identity was protected by law.

It was quite typical for a lesbian couple to both be artificially inseminated by the same anonymous semen donor, thus allowing some relationship between the siblings. Similarly surrogate mothers would carry for two homosexual men.

Dan and Mich had never encountered each other's parents. They had both flown the nest and had moved to another city to study, as most young adults had done before them. Their parents were still a source of comfort for times of stress or sorrow. Luckily for Dan and Mich they hadn't really needed this, the only real time when contact had been made was through social media chat and anniversaries.

The pair of them discussed the possibility of being introduced to each other's parents, or the in-laws as they had jokingly phrased it.

31. Gene Pool

During the 21st Century there was another reason why adoption had become more prevalent, and this was caused by the falling number of births due to various circumstances.

One cause for the low number of conceptions was the falling quota of males with good sperm counts and women with healthy ovaries. This reduction slowly led to the weakening of the human gene pool.

Ovarian reserve measures the ability of a woman's ovaries to produce eggs that will ultimately as an embryo develop into a baby. Whilst age is an important factor, ovarian reserves can be severely affected even in younger women. This decline can occur due to surgery, smoking, cancer treatments, or simply a woman's genetic make-up.

An example of declining birth rates occurred in Japan, where the country's population hit a peak of 128 million in 2010, but shrunk by close to one million in the five years through to 2015, according to census data. Demographers had predicted it would plunge by a third by 2060, to as few as 80 million people — a loss of one million a year, on average. This demise would not be unique to Japan, but eventually would affect Western European countries, and slowly the rest of the world.

There were several factors involved in this decline such as lifestyle, an increase in sexually transmitted diseases, a rise in obesity, and environmental factors such as urbanisation and the urban lifestyle. All of these were contributing to an increase of male and female subfertility.

In addition there were socio-economic factors that led to women and couples delaying having children, including a lack of affordable housing, flexible and part-time career posts for women, and a lack of affordable and publicly funded (free) childcare. With more couples or women in particular delaying starting a family, and with ovarian ageing, this led to a true reduction in fertility levels and resulted in a reduced chance of conception.

Eventually, another new and controversial reason developed that gave cause for birth reduction and gene pool deterioration. It was to do with the sub-conscious mind, the human psyche, it caused this problem to occur towards the latter 21st Century and into the 22nd Century.

Who would have thought that the human subconscious mind could be so powerful?

32. 22ⁿᵈ Century Society

The last few centuries had passed by with the fundamental aspects of life continuing as before.

It's amazing to think that the simple pleasures in life such as eating and drinking have rarely changed over the centuries. Perhaps the only one aspect that changed in this respect was the greater understanding of which foods and drinks provided a healthier diet, and that whilst alcoholic drinks were generally bad for the body and mind, moderation was the key. Fewer people ate meat in general, particularly red meat. More and more people turned to low-fat diets, understanding that a lean body meant a healthier one.

Education would blossom more and more with easier and quicker access to knowledge, enriching the lives of all. Meanwhile, the rich became richer and the poor, whilst becoming poorer, had a better education that allowed them a greater understanding of how to improve their lives. In every walk of life there were always the extremes of morality, from genuine goodness to deceitful greed and evil. Nothing would change this demographic, for this was humanity… sadly.

Religions suffered and diminished at first, but with new scientific discoveries being made all the time, even scientists questioned the new role of religion and so it was re-introduced into society. For every scientific discovery made, a question would be raised as to its origin and existence.

However an amazing change in culture and technology occurred, and a new sociological outlook on life took place.

The late 20th Century saw a change in society. Historically it had been made up of heterosexuals in the main, but now leading politicians, actors, business leaders and others were among those who publicly admitted to being homosexual or bi-sexual.

So in today's epoch around the middle of the 22nd Century, culture and society were dominated by the homosexual community.

Heterosexuals were shunned, considered as lower class and unfit for the higher classes and intellect. The main populace was fed by the media, by community leaders, politicians, actors, comedians, sportspeople and teachers who taught that gay was the way and gay was the norm.

At the beginning of this change, many religions fought hard against the trend, but they knew they were losing the battle.

This homosexual dominance led many heterosexuals to distance themselves from their communities, colleagues and friends, ultimately going underground.

A coming out party was the usual way for those who had found the courage to say they were heterosexual and proud.

It was at this kind of coming out party that Dan and Mich had first met. They had both been good friends with Bobbi, a nickname for Robert, who had fallen for his one true love Henri, short for Henrietta. They had been friends for many years up until the last year, where they had pretended to be platonic, but were secretly meeting to bond closer and closer. Finally they had had enough of the pretence. They knew they would be scorned. They knew they would be persecuted. But they felt that one day this relationship would be accepted in their community and by their families.

With it now being the norm to conform to homosexuality, it also became the fashion to give children gender-neutral names. Over time it was regarded as sexist to give a child a name that was exclusive to either boys or girls.

Examples of popular names were

Jo for Joseph or Joanne / Joanna

Dan for Daniel or Daniella

Mich for Michael or Michaela

Henri for Henry or Henrietta

For many centuries tomboys would give themselves gender-neutral names like Bobbi, for Roberta, or George, for Georgina. They were still feminine in many ways but had a little laddish streak in them. It also paved the way for those who wished to change their sex, something that had occurred over the last few centuries.

33. The Power of the Subconscious Mind

How powerful is the subconscious mind?

How does our brain affect our body and soul?

This was debated by Dan and Mich late one afternoon at the café. The conversation arose because one of Dan's fathers had mentioned the stress he was under at work. A build-up of stress and anxiety eventually led to a series of palpitations or panic attacks.

They were very frightening experiences. Each time, Dan's father believed he was having a heart attack when in reality it was a reaction to falling out of control.

His doctor explained to him that it was caused by the subconscious mind. An almost uncontrollable force that renders the body into a state of shock, causing the heart rate to increase along with adrenalin levels. As a result, the mind effectively flicks a switch to protect the body.

The doctor tried to dismiss the problem by understating the issue. The aim was to sow a seed into Dan's father's subconscious mind, and so avert the alert. But it's not that easy – for it is a very powerful entity!

Dan's father was instructed to stand in front of a mirror and talk to himself. He was to state that there was no issue and that the palpitations or panic attacks would disappear. But, no matter how much his father believed this, his subconscious mind understood that there was still an issue. Therefore the problem continued.

Relaxation music would help a little at first, but slowly after a while the inner consciousness would question why he was listening to this music, and ultimately it knew it was because there was a problem.

Sowing a seed in the subconscious mind was key to diverting attention away from the problem itself. Distraction techniques were used so that the problem could either be buried deep inside or addressed at its source. So the solution was not the relaxation music but possibly lively dance music.

The brain is such a powerful tool. It's not just about knowledge and memory, it also affects the physiology and psychology of the body and mind.

It is common knowledge that exercise releases chemicals in the brain that evoke happiness. Endorphins can be found in the pituitary gland and in other parts of the brain, or distributed throughout the nervous system. They are a type of neurotransmitter, or a chemical messenger that can help relieve pain and stress. They are just one of many neurotransmitters released through exercise. Physical activity also stimulates the release of dopamine, norepinephrine, and serotonin. These brain chemicals play an important part in regulating mood.

Not enough of these chemicals results in the old theory that too much thought or too much self-analysis can bring on depression, causing an imbalance in the body's psychosomatic equilibrium.

It was this power of the inner brain, of the subconscious mind and human psyche that started to impact how the human body behaved and developed when it came to procreation.

As the demographics of society changed between the 21st Century and the 22nd Century, homosexual and asexual relationships meant that the subconscious mind knew there would be no procreation – no natural conception.

Little by little the physical body functions developed away from reproduction. Sperm counts declined, ovarian reserves diminished, the gene pool decreased and the world started to realise there was a problem, although nobody fully understood the reasons.

At first, under-developed countries were encouraged to migrate into western countries to increase the gene pool. This mass migration had occurred for centuries, even during the Iraq and Syrian wars at the beginning of the 21st Century.

But slowly these lesser-developed countries progressed, and so the number of underdeveloped countries dwindled.

Eventually this decimation in the gene pool hit the entire world.

More and more, the world became dependent on IVF treatment.

34. IVF Catastrophe

Towards the end of the 21st Century IVF treatments throughout the world peaked, with millions of babies born every year. However at the beginning of the 22nd Century the number through IVF started to plummet, with the procedure having a high failure rate.

The problem seemed to occur at the point of inserting the embryo into the womb where they were being rejected by the mothers.

The medical institutes were in shock. News spread fast and was covered extensively in the media. What on earth could be causing this catastrophe?

IVF was no longer a treatment for couples struggling to conceive. It was now a standard procedure for those who wanted a surrogate for their new baby. For decades the IVF procedure had been the solution for a high percentage of people wanting a child – but now they had no hope.

Rumours started rapidly that medical institutions were considering the option of human cloning, but there was uproar as the procedure was deemed unethical.

35. Playing God

One of the most controversial methods of procreation, if it can be called procreation, is cloning. Clones are organisms made of exact genetic copies, where every single bit of the clone's DNA is identical to that of another individual.

Clones can happen naturally such as identical twins or can be man-made using cloning techniques in a laboratory.

Natural identical twins can be regarded as both similar to and different from clones made through modern cloning technologies.

Many people first heard of cloning through Dolly the sheep. Dolly was the first known clone. She was created in 1997 at the Roslin Institute in Scotland, although artificial cloning technologies had been around for many years before then.

There are two ways to make an exact genetic copy of an organism in a laboratory, either by artificial embryo twinning or somatic cell nuclear transfer.

Artificial embryo twinning is a relatively low-tech way to make clones. As the name suggests, this technique mimics the natural process that creates identical twins.

In nature, twins form very early in development when the embryo splits in half. Twinning happens in the first days after the egg and sperm join, while the embryo is made of just a small number of unspecialised cells. Each half of the embryo continues dividing on its own, ultimately developing into separate and complete individuals. Since they are developed from the same fertilised egg, the resulting individuals are genetically identical.

Artificial embryo twinning uses the same approach, but it is carried out in a Petri dish instead of inside the mother. A very early embryo is separated into individual cells, which are allowed to divide and develop for a short time in the Petri dish. The embryos are then placed inside the mother, where they finish developing. Again, since all the embryos come from the same fertilised egg, they are genetically identical.

Somatic cell nuclear transfer (SCNT), also called nuclear transfer, uses a different approach to that of artificial embryo twinning, but it produces the same result – an exact genetic copy, or clone, of an individual. This was the method used to create Dolly.

A somatic cell is any cell in the body other than the sperm or egg, the two types of reproductive cells, also called germ cells. In mammals, every somatic cell has two complete sets of chromosomes whereas the germ cells have only one complete set.

The nuclear, or nucleus, is a compartment that holds the cell's DNA. The DNA is divided into packages called chromosomes which contain all the information needed to form an organism. It's the small differences in our DNA that make each of us unique.

To make Dolly, researchers isolated a somatic cell from an adult female sheep. Next, they removed the nucleus and all of its DNA from an egg cell. Then they transferred the nucleus from the somatic cell to the egg cell.

After a couple of chemical tweaks the egg cell, with its new nucleus, was behaving just like a freshly fertilised egg. It developed into an embryo which was implanted into a surrogate mother and carried to term. But this was a problem when working with IVF and so an artificial womb was designed to carry the embryo.

Dolly was an exact genetic replica of the adult female sheep that donated the somatic cell. She was the first-ever mammal to be cloned from an adult somatic cell.

When her creators shared their success with the world it triggered warnings of rich people cloning themselves for spare parts, of tyrants cloning soldiers for armies, of bereaved parents cloning their dead children to produce replacements, and promises that the technique would bring more medical breakthroughs.

Back in 2008 researchers successfully created the first five mature human embryos using somatic cell nuclear transfer (SCNT) where the nucleus of a somatic cell was taken from a donor and transplanted into a vacant host egg cell. The embryos were only allowed to develop to the blastocyst stage, at which point they were studied and then destroyed.

Could there already be clones among us? Could the superrich afford this possibility?

36. The Ethics of Cloning

Throughout the 21ˢᵗ Century the ethics of human cloning were refined. Stem cells can differentiate to become any kind of cell in the body, subsequently they can be utilised for a wide variety of purposes when it comes to treating diseases, particularly genetic diseases, or diseases where a patient requires a transplant from an often elusive perfect match donor. In short, cloning was being used to reproduce replacement body parts in cases of injury or sickness.

In the early 21ˢᵗ Century a woman in Japan suffered from age-related macular degeneration and was treated with induced pluripotent stem (iPS) cells created from her own skin cells. These cells were then implanted into her retinas and the procedure stopped her vision from degenerating further.

Cloning ethics covered a number of issues:

Who would own the copyright? Who would have the right to use the original to clone? And would the original body be able to stop a clone from cloning itself? Could a corporation also claim ownership or copyright, especially if the company invented the method to clone the original?

There is also the potential for someone to clone another individual illegally. All they'd have to do is gather the required biological material, like skin or blood cells, and hire a willing surrogate or use an artificial womb to carry the clone to term. Such an act would be extremely unethical, but not impossible. Biotech labs could do it covertly under a black market, along with cults and religious groups.

It's also possible that parents might want to raise the clone of a child, parent or grandparent who recently passed away, or even clone their favourite pet animal. Ideally, the deceased person would have given prior consent.

Then we come to our main aim in life, immortality, where clones can continue to be cloned indefinitely.

In the early 21st Century researchers in Japan used a new technique to produce over 25 successful generations of cloned mice from one single mouse. In total nearly 600 mice were produced, all of which were genetic duplicates. The breakthrough showed that mammalian cloning lines, including humans, could be extended and reproduced without limit. This implied that a kind of genetic immortality could be achieved; an exact replica of an individual could be copied for no end of generations.

Remember the amoeba?

Dan and Mich had analysed the evolution of Man at key stages and how there were gaps in the humanoid species. So what if in the process of cloning there was a practice of indefinite cloning with selective modifications over time? What if each successive generation could be augmented or altered in specific ways?

A clonal line could feature slow, iterative improvements to intelligence and memory, or changes to physical characteristics, like hair colour or morphology.

Artificial chromosomes could be introduced as they're developed and improved over time by scientists. After centuries of this virtual asexual reproduction, the offspring would scarcely resemble the original version – namely another species of humanoid. Could this be an explanation for why there were gaps in humanoid evolution? Was the DNA of each species manipulated over time with potentially new manufactured chromosomes or genes, by some intelligent civilisation?

37. Eternity

By the end of the 23rd Century humans were trying to live for eternity, or as close to it as possible.

Over the previous centuries, science and discoveries allowed humans to live much longer than had ever been thought possible.

The average age at the beginning of the 21st Century was approximately just over 70 years old, although in certain countries such as Japan this age was approximately 80 years old.

At the same time it is worth noting that a great number of people lived to over the age of 100, particularly in certain places including Costa Rica, Sardinia, Greece and of course Japan. The oldest person on record at the time was a French lady who died at the ripe old age of 122, back in 1997. It's also worth noting that the vast majority of the oldest living people were female.

Scientists announced in late 2017 that they had discovered a rare genetic mutation in an Amish community in Berne, Indiana, that could explain why some members of the group live longer than others.

Amish people in the United States have lived in relative isolation since they emigrated from Europe in the 18th and 19th centuries. It has lent them significant autonomy but has also caused some unique genetic consequences. Centuries of genetic drift and inbreeding left these isolated religious communities with a particular gene mutation that can produce a longer life.

Researchers identified a mutation in the gene, SERPINE1, that is common among the Berne Amish. They discovered that when a person carries only one copy of the mutated SERPINE1 gene, they exhibit some remarkable characteristics associated with longer lifespans as well as longer periods of good health.

The average age rose to 150 by the late 23rd Century while those who lived longer than average would reach the incredible age of 180. It was believed that before too long people would reach 200 years old.

With a greater level of education throughout the world, a healthy diet and regular exercise were commonplace. More importantly, there was more of an understanding of mental health and how the complex brain affected the body.

People's bodies became thinner as they grew taller. The diet had less and less fat content. But this did not mean that society had turned to vegetarianism, for it was recognised that certain meats provided excellent proteins and fibres that aided the body's nervous system. Yes of course there were vegetarians and vegans in increasing numbers, even meat eaters would rarely eat meat, for it was recognised that the body performed better and lived longer as a lean machine.

Society moved towards a cleaner way of living. There was a greater understanding of good and bad bacteria, so much so that the environment became almost sterile and the human body became more immune to viruses and diseases.

More mothers refused to give breast milk to their babies, preferring substitute milk and goodness for fear of passing on bad viruses.

Body and facial hair became taboo, regarded as ugly. It was seen as a breeding ground for bacteria, even though the body needed such hair to aid the respiratory system of the skin.

More and more people wore filters within the nasal and breathing passages to keep out any form of bad bacteria or virus.

The world was more and more shielded from the sun's harmful rays, with a greater emphasis on staying indoors or enclosed arboretums.

In essence the human body became protected on a grand scale.

There were also two major developments:

Firstly, disease was almost eradicated through manipulating bad genes from the body during early conception. Effectively the process of making a baby was becoming more and more scientific and most definitely less romantic.

Secondly, body parts were manufactured from the same stem cells as the host. In effect a clone was made of the original body part. Even parts of the brain could be cloned.

The human body was becoming closer and closer to immortality, due to the ability to build body parts and extend the lifespan of the person.

But in the end it was clear that the human race still needed to procreate.

38. Eradicating Disease

The number of mutations within human DNA is large – by the beginning of the 21ˢᵗ Century these mutations had caused many syndromes and diseases, including different types of cancers, Down's Syndrome and Cystic Fibrosis.

Every time human DNA was passed from one generation to the next it accumulated between 100 to 200 new mutations according to a DNA-sequencing analysis of the Y chromosome.

During the middle of the 21ˢᵗ Century scientists started using a powerful gene-editing tool to fix mutations in embryos, effectively reducing the chance of contracting a disease.

This manipulation of embryos allowed their life expectancy to increase drastically. Furthermore, there were discoveries of genes that prolonged life, allowing cells to regenerate more efficiently. Scientists were starting to invent and create new genes to upgrade the gene pool and enhance the human race and prolong life.

Would they be creating a new species of Man?

Already in the 22ⁿᵈ Century there was a movement towards people having less physical contact with one another due to the implication of passing on bacteria and viruses. Kissing and touching partners was becoming less and less, in fact society was starting to move towards asexuality with more emphasis on intellect and virtual reality.

Virtual reality started way back in the late 20th Century but only really started to develop throughout the 21st Century. It became very real to those who lived their lives by its magic – hypnotised and addicted. The ultimate virtual reality would move away from headsets and goggles, and more towards eye implants tuned into large open spaces, and physically transmitted holograms. There were rumours that technology would continue to progress so that instead of eye implants, humans would see through an area inside the brain that creates the illusion of sight and gives humans their perspective of reality. But this technology was still in the world of science fiction or perhaps science ideology.

In the virtual world Man could run 100 metres in five seconds, Man could travel faster than the speed of light and Man could even fly.

With virtual reality, people were starting to lose their sense of actual reality. For centuries, philosophers had already questioned what reality was. Some would even argue that we already existed in a virtual reality. So what was the truth, and could it be proven?

39. Asexuality

Heterosexuality and homosexuality were already starting to die out, as more emphasis was placed on longevity rather than procreation.

Genitalia through evolution started to reduce in importance. The human psyche began to reduce its size as well as the ability to procreate naturally.

Another form of sexuality started to dominate and that was asexuality, where a person of either gender has no sexual inclination towards any other individual.

As far back as 2001 the Asexual Visibility and Education Network (AVEN) was founded, largely due to the advent of the internet and social media.

In 2009 this new group even participated in the first asexual entry into an American Pride parade as members joined the San Francisco Pride Parade.

By 2010 AVEN even had a flag along the same lines as the LGBT flag, except it did not display a vast array of colours. It had four horizontal stripes, black, grey, white and a dull purple – sad in comparison to the vivacious LGBT flag.

As the end of the 23rd Century approached, people preferred asexual independence.

Any behaviour suggesting sexual intent, even kissing, was regarded as an assault, especially in public. To blow a kiss to someone was considered a crude antisocial gesture or insult. Any public behaviour of this kind would be reported and the individual would be sent to a clinic to undergo therapy.

There was a genuine belief that immortality from procreation, as in passing on genes, was being replaced by immortality through longevity by living a longer life. Philosophers questioned whether this new society encouraged more selfish and detached attitudes in the social network in order to live longer lives.

Great minds were protected in this new age, and were encouraged to live forever. Imagine if the great minds of the past, such as the German Albert Einstein (1879-1955) or the Serbian Nikola Tesla (1856-1943), had lived to a ripe old age of 150? Imagine how much more they would have contributed to science and society, what other discoveries would they have uncovered?

Imagine how a person's passage in time would change? How expectations in life, ambitions and achievements would be affected.

Back in the late 20th Century and early 21st Century the life cycle entailed being born and raised at home until four years of age before embarking on an education system to the age of either 16 or 21 years old, a career to the age of late 60s, maybe even into the early 70s, moving into retirement till death from anywhere between 60 and 100.

The new life cycle at the end of the 23rd Century has the emphasis on early learning. Children start immediately at school, except for very young babies. Once they have reached three years old, they have already been pumped full of information, and even from there it never stops. Education is stretched well towards the end of the 20s. Then follows a career. From there, retirement commences at 90 years, till death at 150, maybe 180 for the lucky ones. This stretching of life expectancy gives rise to many changes in career paths, people would seek other directions, effectively having multiple mid-life crises.

But as the famous song by the rock group Queen goes… Who wants to live forever?

40. A Child's Eye

By the 24th Century, intimacy had become taboo for both adults and children. Children especially were monitored for any such behaviour. If caught, they were immediately sent for reconditioning along with their parents or guardians. Similarly, a formal psychological test was performed prior to a child entering any level of education or social club. This was to ensure that other children could not be influenced.

There was one such little girl called Elle, who at the age of three was already developing into an intellectual young lady. Elle was caught kissing a little boy and her father was instructed to accompany her to a local clinic especially for children. He was allowed to stay with her at all times as she viewed cartoons that were designed to re-condition a child's mind away from sexually-related habits. Since their creation, cartoons have always been used as a way to condition society. They depict how people should look and behave, using subtle hints disguised as entertainment.

The course would take a week. At the end of their conditioning the children would undergo some subtle examinations. Elle's father was an aged man, considered by his peers to be of high intelligence, a man of wisdom. But he found the whole episode of conditioning fundamentally hideous. He vowed to protect his daughter from any such experience in the future. However, he knew that in this society this sterile behaviour would be embedded for a long time to come. He knew what he would have to eventually do and so he sought counsel from his peers.

The rate at which children could soak up information at such a young age was never really understood until the 22nd Century. Before the age of seven children were at the peak of their education. By this early age they could speak multiple languages - this was evident even way back in the 20th Century in cases where parents came from different nations. The emphasis on enhancing this important peak of learning finally reached the education system. The child's brain was like a sponge, soaking in every sense of light, sound and touch. And technology continually enhanced the education system.

But at four, Elle again found herself wanting to kiss and cuddle another boy in her school, except this time she told her father beforehand about what was going on in her head. She seemed to know it was wrong.

One early summer weekend morning Elle's father arranged for her to visit a family friend, who happened to be a doctor. They drove out into the countryside to a large institution. The impressive building, perhaps once an old ancestral home, was located at the end of a mile-long, narrow driveway, lined with tall linden trees.

At the entrance to the property were two enormous wrought iron gates attached to solid stone pillars. Majestic stone dogs lay on the top of each pillar, symbolising their guardianship over the property and the occupants inside. The dogs' heads slightly resembled pharaohs with slightly larger pointed ears than normal. They were sitting in a grand posture signifying that this was a place of importance. In fact it seemed these dogs were a representation of Anubis, one of the most iconic gods of Ancient Egypt. His name is the Greek version, for the Egyptians knew him as Anpu or Inpu. He was an extremely ancient deity whose name is represented as a guardian and protector of the dead and originally a god of the underworld. Later he became the god of mummification for it was Osiris who became the King of the Underworld.

Elle's father drove to a roundabout on which stood a model of a stepped pyramid around three times the height of an average man. The top of the pyramid had been cut off, creating a platform on which people could sit and look out on to the land. It seemed a curious place to install such a monument. But perhaps it symbolised the meaning of the institution, for there did appear to be a number of symbols scattered around this ancestral home.

Finally, Elle's father pulled his car up to the parking area, took a small suitcase out of the boot, and together with his daughter walked up the wide stone steps and entered into the spacious high-ceiling entrance hall. The pair could not but help to stop for a moment in such a hall of grandeur, both scanning the highs and lows of every corner. The hall was covered wall to wall in oil portraits and tapestries. Some seemed to date way back to the 16th Century and even earlier, obviously men and women of great importance in times gone by. The whole entrance hall was made of stone, with corridors in every direction and a majestic set of steps leading to a number of floors.

There were Egyptian God statues surrounding the hall. One in particular had been central to all the others as a pivotal figure. It was on appearance the biggest of all the statues. The god wore a tall conical head-dress narrowing a little at the top and with a smaller oval shaped edge. He appeared to be holding a small crook in his left hand and a small stick with a fan in the other. Elle and her father stood in front of it for a moment admiring its majesty. The receptionist noticed their curiosity and explained that it was a statue of the Ancient Egyptian god Osiris.

Passing around the hall they also spotted a small stone plinth with engravings on it, including what looked like the Sun and its orbiting planets, and a large pharaoh pointing to the stars, as if to convey a message to the observer. It proved to be as fascinating as any museum or exhibition.

Both Elle and her father were asked to wait for a call in the waiting room. It was very much like a typical doctor's waiting area with screens and interactive panels on the walls for people of all ages to read and be entertained. Elle appeared very relaxed and enjoyed playing with the panels whilst her father contemplated the events that might unfold. He seemed to be in a world of his own.

A tall, bald, middle-aged lady dressed all in white came to the door and called their names. They followed her across the entrance hall and into an office whereupon an aging doctor greeted them. The doctor looked incredibly like Elle's father, in fact one could easily have thought they were brothers. Elle noted they seemed to know each other as they chatted about old times. They were like two peas in a pod, with similar gestures and mannerisms.

Elle tried to understand the conversation between her father and the doctor, but she was distracted by the toys in the corner of the room. Even in the 24th Century children still enjoyed physical, tactile toys. Finally Elle was called over to sit on a couch where the doctor started his examination.

At the end of the process the doctor explained that he would like them to return in a couple of days where preparations would be arranged for the next stage. An appointment was subsequently offered to Elle's father.

During the week her father kept dropping hints about going on holiday, somewhere special, somewhere where people and children enjoyed games and cared for each other. A place where one could hold and cuddle friends and family – a wonderful wonderland.

The following week both Elle and her father were sitting, waiting patiently in the doctor's room. The time of this appointment had been very late in the evening, way past Elle's bedtime. But Elle, like any other child, found it exciting to stay up late, even though she was fighting hard not to fall asleep with the occasional yawn here and there.

The father and daughter were shown into a bedroom where they were asked to stay overnight. Elle's father had known about this, so he had brought along a change of clothing as well as their bedtime pyjamas. The doctor popped by to wish them well. He shook Elle's hand and gave her a kiss on the cheek, which surprised Elle. She had not understood the reason, but her father reassured her. The two men shook hands and gave each other a goodbye hug.

The next morning the sun shone through the window and warmed Elle's face. She woke up in what seemed like another bedroom – it just appeared slightly different somehow. It's surprising how very little notice we observe of our surroundings. Elle dismissed this as they both dressed ready to meet the doctor's receptionist.

"Please take this address and flash it into your new vehicle. Your belongings have been transported already, and you should have nothing to worry about.

"Our contact details are here. Please do get in touch if you need anything else or if there's an emergency – but I doubt it.

"Good luck," the receptionist continued. "All of us here wish you well. Goodbye." They shook hands on departure.

As they were leaving the doctor's clinic it became apparent to Elle that she didn't recognise the area from the night before. Even the pyramid had disappeared. Perhaps it was at the rear of the building. This all added to her doubt but her father kept reassuring that they were going on a holiday. She soon forgot about it and started playing on her favourite console as her father drove the car away from the premises and towards the destination for their new life together.

For Elle this was a hugely exciting adventure. Holidays were rare, so to see different environments and new technology she hadn't seen before was tremendous fun, just perfect for a four-year-old.

One day they took a drive out to the seashore, walked in the sand and paddled in the sea. For the first time Elle was able to smell the sweet, salty air and the warm breeze that brushed her hair. They even had a go at making sandcastles, something only done at school in play pits or with virtual reality.

Elle especially had enjoyed the local parks where children had played freely. The park had seen children of her age laughing and crying, hugging and kissing, pushing and kicking. Yes…. even kissing the cheeks of their parents, family and friends. It was the most idyllic place to be. She felt like she was in paradise.

Towards the end of the holiday Elle's father asked her if she would like to move permanently to this region, a place where they had never visited before – this wonderland. Elle's answer was easy as they had had so much fun together. Her reaction was one of glee, with a giggle of joy, as it should be for any happy four-year-old child.

They had found their home.

41. A Ladies' Grudge

It was a beautiful sunny Sunday morning with clear blue skies and the odd scattering of fluffy white clouds. It was idyllic, and for once no rain was forecast – a weatherman's dream.

It was the morning before Brenda's football match. It had been a dry evening with only a little dew on the ground, which made perfect conditions for the event.

The previous night, Braxton and Tina had chatted in bed about what they expected from the game, as neither had actually watched women play before. Tina knew that sport, generally regarded as a pastime for men, had become more and more available to girls and women, including rugby which could be quite physically demanding.

For many years during the 20th and 21st centuries women had fought for equality in sport at all levels. This included fair and equal pay with prize money in some of the more high profile sports such as tennis. Some argued that if women wanted equality then they should compete against men. In some sports this was ridiculous, however in others it was quite possible.

In tennis there were mixed doubles, in horse racing female jockeys competed with men, same for Formula One motorsport, but with football and rugby there was still a gap between the physical elements of the game for a mixed team. Perhaps only fun mixed games were possible, such as charity matches. Women were used as umpires, referees, linesmen or referee assistants in a number of men's sports, and there were more and more female commentators.

But neither Braxton nor Tina had actually watched women play football, nor a ladies' rugby match, and they were intrigued to see how it compared to the men's game.

One reason for playing sport is personal pleasure, including comradery and exercise. Another is for people to watch and take pleasure from a spectator point of view and of course with professional sports it's also about supporting the clubs financially.

Braxton and Tina met up with Gerry and Sally at the bar. They settled down with a beer and ordered their lunch.

"We had a good chat last night about today's game. We're both looking forward to it, though we have no idea really what to expect," Braxton said to Sally and Gerry.

"Funnily enough, so did we. Neither of us has seen a women's game. We kind of expect it to be less aggressive and more polite, we think," replied Gerry. Both Tina and Sally looked at each other and started to laugh.

"What are you laughing at?" asked Braxton.

"Come on guys! You know what women can be like! I wouldn't be surprised if you end up having to run for your lives, playing against this bunch," said Tina.

"Well it's only an amateur game anyway, so we shouldn't be too critical. Let's cheer Brenda on. I'm really looking forward to it, especially the lunch," said Gerry impatiently, waiting for his food.

There was no sign of Brenda or Tracey, but the four of them guessed they were in the changing rooms adjacent to the bar.

"Actually anything could happen and I'm even wondering if the visions in my head might unfold," joked Gerry with a slight grin, looking mainly at Braxton.

"What? You mean a goal is scored and the ladies start kissing each other, and then at the end of the game they start swapping shirts?" replied Braxton, also with a cheeky grin on his face. Both men laughed as Tina and Sally shook their heads in disgust.

"That's just typical of you men! You're so sexist!" remarked Tina. "You should be ashamed of yourselves at your age!"

"Hey! We're not that old! And anyway that's what men do, so it's not that sexist, I think…." Braxton's voice tailored off to nothing and the boys decided to let the subject go.

The kick-off was scheduled for 2pm, so the four decided to stay in the warm, snug bar with another drink and take their time over Sunday lunch. The lunch was a typical carvery with all the trimmings, complete with a traditional pint of beer of course.

There were 10 minutes to go. They paid their bill and wandered over to the side of the football pitch. Everyone was wrapped up tightly with scarves, woolly hats and gloves. Sure enough Tracey stood at the side of the pitch and they marched over to say hello and to give her some company during the game.

Tracey told them how this was actually a grudge match between the top two teams, so they should expect some fireworks during the game. Both Gerry and Braxton thought this sounded excellent as there was nothing like a grudge game to spice up the day.

Both teams were already on the pitch warming up with the odd sprint and zig-zagging runs, practising shots and passing to one another. Brenda's team wore a red and white striped kit whereas the opponents were all in blue.

Braxton remarked how some of the ladies were quite beautiful and feminine. Tina shot him down as one would a teenager. "For goodness sake, Braxton, what were you expecting? They're not all butch! And even if they were, it's their lives! They can each choose how they want to live. Start behaving like an adult!"

Braxton made comments about two attractive ginger players. "What do you think, Tina? Should we bring Joe along next time? There are two lovely ginger-haired girls in Brenda's team. Do you think Joe's got a chance? I still haven't found him a young lady yet. He did say he preferred red-haired girls."

"Well, let's come to the next game and bring him along. Although we perhaps ought to ask Brenda or Tracey if he stands a chance," smiled Tina with a wink.

Braxton couldn't help but notice that some of the women were continually chomping on chewing gum or spitting on the ground, some were even wiping their noses across their sleeves. For some reason he just simply hadn't expected this, he kind of equated these actions to men's behaviour. It was as if the players were mimicking the professionals on TV, but then thinking about it, isn't that what children and men do in amateur games? So it shouldn't come as a shock. There's nothing new there and it's quite normal to mimic your heroes.

From the moment of kick-off both Gerry and Braxton could see that this was indeed a very physical game with some pretty aggressive tackles. It was evident that it wouldn't be long before a fight would flare up. Braxton and Gerry were loving it and both Tina and Sally seemed enthralled in the game too.

Even Tracey, who previously seemed a very reserved kind of person, found her vocal chords, screaming at the top of her voice for the team to "Get stuck in!"

"Wow! This is really entertaining, Gerry, especially now we know it's a grudge game. It's almost as good as the real thing!" cried out Braxton.

Sure enough, there was one hard tackle too many and before long two of the women were on the ground with fists flying. Braxton could have sworn that one of them threw a head-butt.

"Oh, my! This really is intense," shouted Braxton.

"Go on! Give it back!" screamed Tracey.

"You know, Gerry, I think I just heard the pair of them swear at each other," remarked Braxton.

"Ah come on, Braxton, don't be an idiot! How many times have you heard me curse and swear at you? You're joking, right?!" Tina was not happy with Braxton.

"Yeah, sure! No, I was just joking and didn't mean to offend. Yes, of course, it's only natural. Sorry," said Braxton apologetically, as Gerry looked at him with a smirk on his face.

"Hell, you two are like a pair of schoolboys! Stop it!" Sally barked at them whilst checking that Tracey had not overheard.

Braxton and Gerry looked at each other in total surprise, both thinking that from this day forward they would see women in a different light. They had been enlightened and suitably scolded.

The game ended as a nil-nil draw, but it was certainly not boring, with a number of fights and brawls. There had also been a fair amount of spitting, which Braxton had found a bit off-putting.

Brenda had a relatively quiet game, managing to get into fisticuffs just the once. Fortunately, despite all the aggression, there were no major accidents or injuries that came out of the game. Tracey informed the four of them that the matches weren't usually this violent. It was simply that both teams hated each other. This was due to a previous meeting that ended up in one major brawl. Braxton and Gerry could quite believe it and were grateful not to be playing in such a game.

After the match the four of them, along with Tracey, met up at the bar so they could thank Brenda for an entertaining afternoon. Brenda seemed pre-occupied and agitated, perhaps it was due to the intensity of the rivalry. She also looked very pink in the face having just come from the changing rooms and showers.

Apparently it seemed that the scoreless draw suited the other team which had a marginal one-point lead at the top of the league. Brenda was confident that they would beat them next time. "We'll kick 'em off the park!" were her exact words, with Tracey by her side nodding in support.

Normally the visiting opposition would stay after the game for a quick drink with the hosts, but such was the animosity between the two teams that both coaches agreed it was best for the visitors to head home directly from the dressing rooms.

When Brenda eventually calmed down, she and Tracey announced that Tracey was pregnant. Brenda was looking forward to becoming a father to Tracey's baby. They all celebrated with a round of drinks.

Braxton was never too sure how to address same sex couples, especially those with children. Should women be called mothers or can a woman call herself a father? Likewise could one of the two men call themselves a wife or mother? Perhaps this was down to the individuals themselves.

Braxton noticed that both Gerry and Sally had been a little quiet following the news. The fact that they had been trying for a baby for over two years, only to hear an announcement from Tracey and Brenda about their baby, must have touched a nerve. "Are you OK, Gerry? Did you hear any news about your IVF?" asked Braxton.

"Oh don't worry, Braxton, we're OK," said Gerry in appreciation. "We're very happy for Tracey and Brenda, of course we are. We'll get there too, eventually, it's just a matter of time. We'll just have to be patient, that's all. But thanks for asking. Good to know you're thinking of us." Gerry gazed over towards Sally and they smiled knowingly towards each other.

After a while, Braxton mentioned that he might bring his brother Joe to the next home match. Joe enjoyed a good game of football. He was also very partial to redheads, and of course Braxton had noticed the two redhead girls in the team. "What do you think, Brenda? Tracey?" quizzed Braxton.

"Oh, you mean Emma and Emily?" said Brenda, with a smile on her face. "Oh yes, bring him along. They're sisters you know, and they are into boys. Perhaps a bit shy, but we'll help you, Braxton. Should be fun.

"Let's see now," Brenda added. "Our next home game is actually next week, next Sunday. So why don't we meet up at the bar before the game? I'll have a word with Emma and Emily, and I'm sure they would come." Brenda spoke with total confidence.

"We'll see you at the quiz night then, shall we?" said an excited Tracey.

"Oh yes, without fail," said Tina.

"OK, then, we'll see you all on Wednesday!" Both Brenda and Tracey walked out of the bar leaving the two couples to have a final drink for the road.

"See! I told you they're not all lesbians or butch! The two girls sound lovely. You'd better tell Joe to get a decent haircut while you're at it!" smirked Tina to Braxton.

"Yes, and a shave!" concluded Braxton, and all four of them laughed.

The next day Braxton called Joe over for a beer. They sat down as Braxton described the events of the ladies football match. Braxton explained how he had been quite shocked at some of the antics, commenting on some of the attractive ladies in both teams, at which point Joe's ears pricked up.

"Yes, and I have to say, Joe, there were two gorgeous looking redheads on Brenda's team. Perfect for you! Similar age, and they're into boys too!" said Braxton with a glint in his eye.

"Sounds good, Braxton. Do you think I would be able to come to the next game?"

"I thought that might interest you. Oh, I would say so. Both Tina and I will also go to keep you company. We enjoyed the game the other day and thought it was very entertaining in many ways," said Braxton.

"But, we think you might need to smarten yourself up a bit. Get a haircut! And maybe a shave at the same time. You look a scruff!" ordered Braxton.

"Seriously?" Joe seemed quite hurt, but realised on reflection that his brother was probably right. "Sure, I'll see what I can do." And he gave a wink to Braxton.

42. Le Café

Both Dan and Mich had regularly frequented the café close to the university campus, but until now had never met each other. Truth be told, both of them had only ever really paid attention to the friends they were with, rather than others around them. If they had arranged to meet a friend they would seek that person out, not really paying attention to anyone else. They may have even previously walked past each other like ships in the night. Nevertheless they were both familiar with the café.

They each headed towards their corner table in the café as they arrived.

"Sorry I'm late, Mich!" exclaimed Dan.

"You're not late, Dan, and it wouldn't matter if you were – not in the grand scheme of things."

"OK, what do you want to drink? My treat!" Dan was perhaps trying too hard. He had no need to.

"My usual Dan, a grand café!"

"Wow! That sounds fantastic! What is it?" asked Dan.

"It's a large coffee."

"And I'll have a Café Olé!" said Dan, clicking his fingers like a castanet. "That's a Spanish coffee," he added, and they laughed.

Some days you would find Dan at the corner table, sitting with his back to the wall. His knees would be up with his feet on the next chair, and he would be holding a sketchpad and pencil. He would survey the clientele and sketch the scene, or certain characters he had found of interest. He wondered how one could go about finding a job as a courtroom sketch artist. He enjoyed the rapid sketch, for there was a certain anticipation over whether the drawing would come close to the real thing. Dan had honed this skill impressively.

Often, when walking into the café, Mich would find Dan in the corner and on most occasions she would jokingly enquire about any cranium sketches.

The owner of the café was an art fan. In fact, close to where Dan and Mich would regularly sit, there was a copy of a famous painting by an American artist, Edward Hopper, called Nighthawks. It depicted a café with large windows. Quite ironic really, as it reminded the owner of Dan and Mich as they sat with their coffees, looking out of their large window. The owner suggested he might be able to display some of Dan's better sketches for his clientele to enjoy. Perhaps Dan could even try to sell some of them to supplement his university grant.

43. Something More

Dan and Mich's relationship started on a platonic footing. There was something in their spirituality and closeness such that the more they saw each other, the more pleasurable it became. It was not unnatural to have a platonic friendship between men and women in these times. Friends are friends and this would never change in any epoch.

Mich enjoyed Dan's world of art. Meanwhile, Dan loved to delve into Mich's world of history. He would be overwhelmed at how Man had continued to evolve to the point where one could live how one lives today.

Both of them found pleasure in Dan sketching Mich, especially if she was nude. Mich always felt totally relaxed, knowing Dan's appreciation of her body and soul through his art. Mich could see Dan's enthusiasm whenever she shared her knowledge on the various periods of history. He loved her voice and often wished her stories would never end.

In the early 21st Century it was a trend for men to shave their heads. Often they shaved after developing a small bald patch. By shaving their heads they hoped to make themselves look young again.

Today in the 22nd Century many women also sported bald heads, or very short-cropped hair. This included popular fashion and perfume models, as well as film stars. It became part of the clean image, of class and refinement.

Of course, due to her alopecia, Mich had favoured the bald look. And Dan couldn't help but feel attracted to it. There was something sensual, almost naked, and he couldn't stop staring at her. He was so enthralled by her look, that it wasn't long before he too shaved his head. Together they made the perfect pair as friends and secret lovers.

On one occasion, Mich invited Dan to join her in visiting her father who lived an hour's drive from the city in a small town. Dan was honoured although quite nervous at the thought. They planned the visit in advance and made their way across the city and on to her father's home. It turned out to be a small modest house.

Her father could not have been a better host. He greeted Dan like he was his own son, embracing him with complete affection. They took their bags into Mich's bedroom, which made Dan feel a little awkward, as the times were against such heterosexual behaviour. Somehow, Mich's father seemed to embrace it. All three went for a walk and chatted about the town. Mich's father also talked about how Mich was so studious at school when she was younger. He also spoke of her friends and where they were now. Mich and Dan continued their walk, while her father made his way home to make supper. When no-one was around, they would either hold hands or Dan would walk with his arm lovingly around her.

They passed a playground. It was the playground that Mich had so much affection from her earliest memories. She explained to Dan how she adored her time there when she was a child and told him of how it filled her with memories of love and happiness.

Surprisingly, Dan felt the same. For some strange reason he also seemed to recognise the playground and surroundings. He also seemed to have the same warm feelings. It felt so weird, as if he had also been here. It was like a vague distant memory, unlocked for the first time. But that was absurd, it couldn't have been, so he dismissed it and continued to listen to Mich's stories. How he loved to hear her voice.

They arrived home in time for supper. Mich's father had prepared a lovely meal and together they discussed their studies, or what they wanted to be when they grew up, as Mich's father had jokingly put it. The evening arrived and Mich's father bid them goodnight. He retired to his slumber with a hug for Dan, followed by an embrace and a big kiss for his daughter.

The room fell silent as Dan and Mich gazed at each other, taking advantage of their freedom, alone together, facing the reality of how much they cared for each other. Dan shed a little tear as he explained to Mich how much he loved her, and in return Mich stroked his cheek tenderly, as if to wipe his tear and return her love. They embraced, and arm in arm they climbed the stairs to their bedroom where they spent the night in their cocoon of love.

The following morning Dan and Mich enjoyed a hearty breakfast with her father. They thanked him for such a relaxing and memorable visit. They packed their belongings, and returned to their university digs as a new couple, completely entwined, completely as one, focused as one. It was as wonderful as could be, for they would not have believed they would feel such euphoria together.

Together, they had started a new chapter in their lives.

44. Trip to the Zoo

Mich and Dan decided to spend the day at the local zoo. But this was no ordinary zoo. It was one of several around the world that specialised in previously extinct animals, hence its name Extinct Zoo.

The first of such zoos opened in the latter part of the 21st Century to mixed reaction – just as cloning had received a mixed reaction when it started way back in the 20th Century. When the zoos originally opened, there were only a few different species on view. So while the visits were brief, the incredible emotions and significance of such an establishment were enormous.

Over the years more extinct zoos opened across the globe. With every new opening each zoo was home to a greater diversity of mammals and reptiles than the previous. They were hugely popular and attracted funding from every sector. While the zoos had serious implications, including the fact that these creatures had been revived out of extinction, their concept also embellished fun and excitement on a par with theme parks such as Disneyland.

Mich and Dan's day out at the Extinct Zoo finally arrived. The weather report was excellent with sunshine forecast for the whole day. Both had an idea of which species would be on view, having checked on the internet. On the way there Mich talked about the amazing and beautiful tigers that had been lost to the world, whilst Dan couldn't wait to see the gigantic and hairy woolly mammoth. They also wanted to see the famous dodo, located in the birds' section.

The dodo had always been everyone's favourite. It had existed on the island of Mauritius and became extinct in the 17th Century. Since then it had been used to symbolise all creatures that had become extinct. It appeared as a character in the story of 'Alice's Adventures in Wonderland' and had a reputation of being fat and clumsy.

Mich and Dan paid their entrance fees, bought their zoo programme, and continued to discuss other amazing creatures that had been awakened from extinction.

In the programme there was a map illustrating how the zoo had been sectioned into areas. Each area housed certain mammals and reptiles, of which these were broken down further into categories for each species. There was a section for cats, another for elephants and mammoths... the list went on, as the number of revived species was vast and diverse. Information panels detailed illustrations and included the creatures' extinction dates. As part of the theme park entertainment staff dressed as caricatures of the creatures. These characters were designed especially for children to enjoy and, perhaps secretly, the adults too.

In almost all the extinct zoos throughout the world there were no dinosaurs. There were reptiles and some experts would say that some of the slightly larger reptiles were in fact dinosaurs. Sadly, there were no Tyrannosaurus rex, nor velociraptors, for obvious reasons. Imagine trying to protect the public with such violent predators! It would be like Jurassic Park! However, it was said that the Extinct Zoo just outside Tokyo, Japan, was more interested than any other in housing such awesome creatures. There was talk, although maybe it was just a rumour, of cloning a Tyrannosaurus! Perhaps this affection for dinosaurs stemmed from the Japanese's obsession with Godzilla.

Today the zoo was very busy, probably because it was the weekend and there had been a number of advertisements in the media.

Mich and Dan decided to follow the route designed to pass each section, even though there were shortcuts throughout the zoo pathways.

The starting section covered a number of small to medium sized mammals.

The first on view was the quagga. Mich and Dan's first reaction was to smile at each other, for as Dan phrased it: "It looks like the quagga has had someone glue the front half of a zebra to the rear half of a horse! In fact maybe the guys with the sophisticated blowtorch were at it again!" Mich smiled in agreement. The pair read the panel in front of them. The quagga sadly became extinct in the 19th Century, having lived in South

Africa, and took its name from the sound it made. It was finally hunted to extinction in 1883. It seemed relatively tame, allowing visitors to stroke the back of its neck, the same as any tame horse or pony would have done.

"Welcome back, my friend!" Mich said to the quagga.

"Hear, hear!" agreed Dan, as he put his arm around her. It was a touching moment.

This was a common phrase heard throughout the zoo, along with other such expressions as "I'm so sorry we caused your extinction, my friend," or, "We won't let you go away again… we promise!"… True sentiments indeed.

It was also quite typical to find others in tears – men and women alike. This was due to the realisation and the enormity of seeing these revived creatures in all their beauty, and the understanding that their extinction was most likely caused by Man.

In the family Elephantidae section there was of course the lost elephants and woolly mammoth. A popular beast, the mammoth had been characterised in numerous cartoons and animations, including the movie Ice Age at the beginning of the 21st Century. The panel explained how the creature had existed in the Pleistocene Epoch and had died out in around 2000 B.C. There was a little detail about the movie and a quick reference to his extinct friend the sabre tooth tiger, which was to be found in among the cats.

They arrived at the Felidae section to see the cats and were suitably impressed with the scale of the sabre tooth tiger, also known as a smilodon. The smilodon became extinct way back in around 10000 B.C., so the zoo was incredibly fortunate to have brought it back from extinction. It had characteristic huge canines protruding from its enormous and powerful jaw, and more impressively was its height to its shoulders which must have been well over a metre and a half.

"Wow, what a beast!" exclaimed Dan.

"Yes, built more like a bear than a tiger!" agreed Mich.

In an adjacent area was the Tasmanian Tiger, an animal that became extinct in the 1930s due to farmers hunting it down for fear of attacks on their livestock. Dan and Mich read that it was in fact a marsupial, and bizarrely both the male and female had a pouch. It was nearly two metres in length, and again Dan couldn't help but notice that the animal appeared to be a hybrid.

"Hey Mich, look at that, this is another animal with two parts. Looks like someone's glued the back of a tiger to the head of a fox! Maybe the guys with that fancy blowtorch have been at it again – welding and manipulating species!" joked Dan.

"Yes, I see what you mean now," said Mich with a wink, as they laughed together.

Finally, Mich and Dan arrived at the bird section, and already around the corner they could see Dodi and Dido – a male and female caricature of the dodo. They were of course two adults dressed up in dodo costumes, swamped by young children and adults alike, both constantly posing for photographs and giving the children hugs. Mich and Dan had a photo taken of the both of them posing either side of the two birds, creating a souvenir of their day out together.

The visit took a good six hours, and with the heat of the sun, the young couple were fatigued as they returned home. Both had found the experience very emotional. They couldn't help but think that these species had been given a second chance in their evolution, without even knowing it. Could one say the same about the human race? Had the human race been given a second chance, once upon a time in the distant past?

45. A Ladies Match

Sunday arrived, Joe met Braxton and Tina at their house and together they walked to the local bar to meet the others. Both Braxton and Tina were looking forward to their dinner, while Joe couldn't wait to meet the ginger-haired sisters. He hadn't slept the night before due to his potential new adventure. He almost felt as though he was on a blind date, a double blind date in fact, as the anticipation gave him butterflies in his stomach.

"What are they like, Braxton?" quizzed Joe, who had already conjured up an image or two in his mind.

"Oh, slim, quite tall, very pretty, wouldn't you say Tina?" Braxton looked at Tina with a wink.

"Ah, yes, very pretty. You can tell they are sisters, for sure. There can't be much difference in age either Joe, they must be about the same as you. They have lovely hair, a beautiful warm auburn, actually, quite long too. They each had their hair tied back in a ponytail, as I remember. Not so sure there's much more to say, really. We haven't met them properly yet, so we'll be meeting them for the first time just like you." Tina didn't really offer much more information.

"I can't wait!" cried Joe, clenching his fists in euphoria.

Braxton and Tina smiled at each other, content in the knowledge that Joe was happy in his excitement.

The threesome arrived at the bar before the others and settled down with a beer. They decided not to order their food until the others had arrived. It wasn't long before Brenda and Tracey entered the bar, followed by the two sisters Emily and Emma.

They all stood up for the introductions, with handshakes or kisses on cheeks.

Both Emily and Emma had their long shoulder-length, wavy red hair loose in all its glory – like glowing flames. They seemed to know that their hair was attractive, and knew how to flaunt it, especially after being introduced to Joe.

The twins also made no effort to dress differently. They seemed to wear the same type of clothing, content with the same fashion and dress sense.

Joe couldn't help but notice they were both in tight jeans with the same pink coloured sweatshirts. In fact, Joe was trying desperately to spot differences between the two so that he didn't embarrass himself, concentrating hard on which one was Emily and Emma.

Both sisters commented on how Braxton and Joe were ginger-haired. Quite ironic really, since both lads had also talked about nothing else when discussing the two sisters.

"Yes, well, you're red-haired too! Guess it runs in your family as well, being sisters. Are your parent's ginger?" Joe was in total awe of the sisters.

"No, our dad is dark-haired, although when he grows a moustache or beard it's ginger. But our mother is a real dark auburn redhead, and we're not just sisters but identical twins!" replied Emily.

"Wow! Twins!" said Joe with perhaps too much enthusiasm, and the girls giggled as if they received this reaction every time.

Very quickly, as if to distract the twins from the embarrassment of Joe's enthusiasm, Tina said: "We thought you were of similar age when we watched the match last week. But now you mention it – close up, yes you really are identical, aren't you!"

"We're a dying breed, you know," said Emma.

"Who? You mean twins?" asked Joe.

"No, ginger-nuts. You know, redheads. We're becoming less and less as generations pass. Only a decade ago it was thought we would be wiped out by 2060," qualified Emma.

"Oh, I didn't realise that. I see redheads everywhere... almost all of the time. So I'd never have thought that would be the case. Oh well, then we should all stick together, don't you think?" said Joe.

"Totally, Joe! Let's keep the redhead tribe going!" shouted Emma as she playfully placed her hand on Joe's knee. Emily laughed, while Joe blushed. He wasn't quite sure what they meant by that. Was she proposing a date in some way? He hoped so.

"Let's toast to redheads everywhere. Long may we live forever!" proposed Joe, and all seven grinned as they clinked each other's glasses.

"Cheers! To redheads!" they all cried out in unison.

Finally, the time came for Emily, Emma and Brenda to change for the match. Joe didn't want to give up so quickly, so he invited the twins to the quiz night on Wednesday. Braxton shot a look at Joe as if to say they didn't need his services. But then he realised that perhaps they could invent a story; that one of the team might not be able to make it, or that they needed a rest for a week. The twins thought it was an excellent idea and agreed to meet up on the night. In the mean time they were also keen to meet up again at the end of the match, after what they hoped would be an easy victory.

Joe was relieved that he would be seeing them both at least twice. He was like a love-struck teenager all over again.

Unlike the last game, the football match passed by with no incident. It was very much as Tracey had said, the previous one really must have been a grudge match. Braxton couldn't even remember one fiery incident in this game – quite tame really. The only amusing part was watching Joe who couldn't take his eyes off the twins, as he ran along the touchline giving them every encouragement.

The game ended as predicted, with Brenda's team winning 2-0. Emma scored one of the goals, from which one could see Joe desperately tempted to run on the pitch to give her a celebratory hug and kiss. Fortunately, to the relief of Braxton, Joe refrained and kept his dignity.

After the match they all met up for a quick drink and once more confirmed plans to see each other at the quiz night. Joe mentioned to Braxton that he was thinking of forming his own team with the twins. They just needed another redhead, maybe his friend, Glyn. Perhaps they would call themselves The Carrot Tops.

Braxton was also now intrigued about the claim that redheads were a dying breed. He decided to research this phenomenon.

46. Ginger Nuts and Carrot Tops

When Braxton arrived home, he went straight on the internet to research the news that redheads were dying out. He had heard this rumour before, but hadn't given it much thought as most of his family were redheads, and they also seemed quite common in his circles.

Braxton found that in 2007 many news organisations reported that redheads, or gingers, would eventually become extinct. Other news outlets and social media also claimed that there would be no more redheads by as early as 2060.

It turned out that all these people were wrong, for redheads were here to stay and should still be around as long as humanity exists.

Red hair had long been associated with Celtic people. Both the Ancient Greeks and Romans described the Celts as redheads. There are other areas of the world including Germanic countries such as Holland, and Scandinavian countries such as Denmark, that have red hair. They all have a common ancestry that can be traced back to a single Y-chromosomal haplogroup: R1b.

This colouration is caused by a mutation in the MC1R gene, which is located on chromosome 16, or the melacortin-1 receptor. This is a receptor that when stimulated makes the skin cells, or melanocytes, produce more pigment called melanin. There are two types of pigment in the skin: eumelanin and pheomelanin.

Redheads have more pheomelanin which causes the reddish pigment.

It's also a recessive trait. This means that it takes both parents to pass on a mutated version of the MC1R gene to produce a redheaded child. Because it's a recessive trait, red hair can easily skip a generation, but it can then reappear if both parents, no matter their hair colour, carry the red hair gene.

People born with red hair are part of a genetic minority group with a passionate pride. The unique feature makes them special and almost part of an exclusive club. Less than one per cent of the world population has naturally red hair. The exception is in Scotland and Ireland, where more than one in 10 people are red headed.

Redhead Day started in the Netherlands with a festival called Roodharigendag. It takes place every first weekend in September in the city of Breda in the Netherlands. Taking its cue from this event, the celebration of red hair has spread around the world with the first Saturday of September becoming an international celebration of redheads.

Brittany in France is another region famous for redheads. It too has a venue to hold this great event, called Le Festival de Roux. In the last week of August, thousands of redheads converge on a small town called Orgères, south of Rennes.

Braxton checked to see if such an event existed in England, and sure enough found one in London, held every year in the middle of May.

Braxton felt proud to be a redhead and told Joe so. Who knows, maybe one September day they would visit Breda to celebrate their clan. Maybe in August to Brittany. Or pop on a train to London in May. He started to formulate an idea – perhaps they could go to a different venue each year!

47. Sport and Leisure

Sport had seen a number of changes between the early 21st Century and the 22nd Century. Physical sports, in particular, were re-regulated with new rules. Such rules included banning any physical contact, as far as was possible, or at least introducing more protection, especially to the head.

All physical sports were now touch only, which apart from being extremely difficult to enforce, didn't really enhance them from a spectator's point of view. These medically enforced decisions had not been taken lightly, as there was a trade-off between safety and commercialism. At the end of the day, it was the paying customer who drove the market and the final product.

One can imagine in both professional and amateur sports there is always a sense of bending the rules and pushing the limits. There is always a grudge or someone with an aggressive nature. Of course accidents will always happen, or at least appear to.

Science and technology continued to advance in the sports industry pushing physical constraints even further. As a consequence, men and women continued to break records, to run faster, jump higher – and so it continued. But who knows at what point these records would cease to be broken. There had to be a point at which humans had reached their limits, surely? For example could we imagine a man running the 100 metres in five seconds? Of course not! That would be ridiculous!

Women also started to narrow the gap between themselves and men in performance and strength. Eventually there really was an argument for a complete mixed game in all sports.

Mich and Dan often enjoyed a simple game of badminton together. It was a gentle and seemingly harmless sport, ideal for the winters as it was played indoors. During the summer months they would sometimes play tennis. Playing sport gave Dan a great excuse to see Mich in a skirt, she had such a sexy body. Meanwhile, Mich could see Dan in his shorts. He had such a muscular and sinewy form.

They started out with the odd game here and there, but after a while decided to join a local club and book in some coaching lessons. Finally they started playing as a mixed couple in both badminton and tennis competitions. They loved every minute of it, spending more and more time together and even winning the odd match or two.

They enjoyed the after game get-togethers at the club's sports bar, although their favourite tipple would be a hot lemon tea in the winter, or iced tea in the summer.

These sporting events gave Dan and Mich the opportunity to meet with other mixed couples who were equally sporty. They also bonded with people who had an underlying feeling of friendship and sexual attraction within the heterosexual social network, a similar inclination to heterosexuality in a subtle way, under the guise of sport.

They regularly played friendly matches against a couple called Jack and Bill, or Jacqueline and William. They would also play against their old friends Bobbi and Henri, whose coming out party was where Dan and Mich first met. It had become quite a social group where secretly they called themselves the Hetero Club.

48. Touch Football

Dan also loved to play football, it had been his favourite sport since the age of two. There was something about the skill of working the ball, scoring a goal, sprinting past an opponent, winning matches, and team bonding. He had been developing his skills ever since he could remember.

He played as a striker up front, always wearing the number nine shirt, and he loved scoring goals. There was no greater thrill of hitting the back of the net with the ball.

Mich tried to encourage Dan by watching him from the sidelines whenever she was available, come rain or shine. She gained as much pleasure in watching Dan have fun, as Dan himself had while playing the game.

Modern day football had changed as a sport. It had become almost contactless, and so timing was very important when it came to tackling. One only had to simply misjudge a tackle, and a free kick would be awarded. In fact, at times, many felt the game had been spoiled by interruptions and stoppages because there were so many free kicks.

In the early 21st Century, it became apparent that heading a football was a major cause of dementia. As a result, heading was banned. This ban was enforced within schools after analysis showed it was most damaging to be heading the ball during a child's growing phase. Eventually there were also attempts to ban it in the adult game.

In reality this rule was very difficult to regulate. All the referee could do was award a free kick, but after a number of trials, the rule was scrapped.

Advances in technology meant that the ball became more of a balloon than the previous old leather bound fabrication. Even back in the mid-20th Century there were the old thick leather balls tied up with shoelaces that could cut open a player's forehead. The balloon became more unpredictable in mid-flight which made it more interesting, if not awkward for the players to judge. But it was just as entertaining all the same.

Eventually both women and men played alongside each other on the same teams, and in many cases the women were perhaps more physical and aggressive than the men.

At first the men were unsure how to handle their new team-mates, perhaps treating the women with too much respect and gentleness. But this delicate situation soon changed after a few hardy tackles made the men realise that they were in for a physical game. The women would be particularly aggressive. Eventually rules would state a minimum number of women in the club's squads and a minimum number of women selected in a team. This provided equality across all teams in a league. The mixed game progressed early in the amateur leagues but struggled at the top professional level with hardened traditionalists favouring a purist sport.

49. Joe's Theory

Joe popped over one evening for a catch up over a chilled beer or two with Braxton and Tina. As usual he couldn't help but discuss his latest theories, which at times made good material for Braxton and Tina at the quiz night, or even for Braxton's work related research.

"The geometrics of the pyramids are too precise. The stones of the pyramids are too large to manipulate. The alignments with celestial bodies and the Magnetic North Pole are beyond belief. So it's impossible to believe that the pyramids were built by our ancestors. It's so obvious, isn't it!" Joe exclaimed,

"I don't know, Joe. Is it?" said Tina, half listening, whilst Braxton went to get the beers from the fridge.

"But, of course! These pyramids were built by people who had superior technology from alien visitors thousands of years ago!" Joe continued.

"Rubbish!" shouted Braxton as he entered the lounge with three cans of beer.

"Just look at the evidence!" Joe was adamant as he reached for one of the cans from Braxton.

"What evidence?" Tina sat forward, as if to show interest.

"Well there are two diagonal lines extending from the pyramids on either side of the Nile River Delta. The early Egyptians could not have known this when they were built.

"So, a couple of aliens flew high enough over the Earth to be able to see where the Nile Delta's origin was positioned. They easily saw what orientation the pyramid would need to be in order for its diagonals to lie on those two lines.

"Also, the Great Pyramid lines up almost exactly with the Magnetic North Pole. So how could the Egyptians possibly have built their pyramid facing the exact Magnetic North Pole without even having a compass?

"Those aliens, abundant in their knowledge and drowning in technology, came along and using their compasses, they landed on Earth and found the actual magnetic north and south poles. Then they built the pyramids."

Braxton and Tina looked at each other almost believing that Joe had been sniffing glue or something. "Come on, Joe, don't you think this is all a little bit far-fetched?"

"Well, how come the pyramids were built so mathematically perfect to align with celestial objects? It simply would not have been possible for our early ancestors to achieve this!" insisted Joe.

To support his arguments, Joe opened his laptop and started to show a photograph of the Great Pyramid of Giza and its neighbour, as seen from the sphinx on the evening of the Summer Solstice.

"The Sun is seen setting in the exact centre of the two pyramids. At the time, the Egyptians did not know the exact length of the year, or when the Summer Solstice occurred," explained Joe. "Aliens, however, would have been able to calculate the longest day of the year."

"The Sun also rises and traces the head of the sphinx on the Winter Solstice.

"The positioning of the three pyramids of Giza are aligned exactly with the three stars in the Belt of Orion, as they were in 10500 BC. Therefore aliens, with their wisdom, came down in the year 10500 BC and built the pyramids and the sphinx!

"They built the sphinx with the head of a lion to match the Belt of Orion, as well as the constellation of Leo. Thousands of years later, Khufu, the pharaoh of Egypt, decided that he didn't like having the head of a lion on top of the statue in his land. So he had a head constructed which resembled his own likeness.

"The date of 10500 BC denoted the beginning or First Time of the Age of Leo. This was when the lion constellation would have risen at dawn before the Sun on the day of the Spring Equinox. This event brought the celestial lion to rest due east, thus in perfect alignment with the sphinx.

"The sphinx, in other words, was made to look at his own image on the horizon - and consequently at his own 'time'. Here then were not just the pyramids but also the sphinx luring us to the same date of 10500 BC.

"There's no way this could have been done by the people of the time, it all points to the obvious," Joe concluded as Braxton went off to fetch another beer.

Joe waited for Braxton to sit down again. This little break would also give Braxton and Tina time to reflect on this information. He wanted to shock them… "And that's not all…" Both Braxton and Tina turned and looked Joe in the eye – waiting for the finale. "They've discovered a pyramid on Mars!" Braxton and Tina turned to each other and burst out laughing.

"I'm serious! It's true! Look!" Joe started showing the pyramid and the formation of buildings close by that supposedly existed on the Red Planet.

Joe went on to show the face of a human looking down on the surface from an orbiting space craft. With clever mirroring of the image, the researchers were able to conjure up the face of a lion. Was there a link to the sphinx in Egypt?

The problem today is that with the latest technology everything we see in photographs and images could be manipulated. One has only to look at the latest sci-fi movies to see how incredible and how real the imagery looks. In a way it's quite sad that if there were any truth in any of these conspiracies, people will always question whether the imagery has been manipulated. It's also such a shame that these completely ridiculous conspiracies are casting doubt on those which are truly real.

50. Alien Visitors and Crop Circles

"OK, Joe, so what you are saying is that the sphinx and the pyramids were built by aliens? Braxton wanted to confirm Joe's thoughts. "So, why? What's the point?

"With the pyramids, no-one is certain what their purpose was. Even now they are finding shafts and channels that don't seem to have a function. Although the current theory is that they were huge power stations.

"But I think that's just part of the jigsaw. One of many clues, leaving a trail of their existence for those that will eventually understand."

"Understand what, Joe?" Braxton felt like he was interrogating a subject in a crime investigation.

"That we are not alone. That when we are ready we will all be together sharing the same world," continued Joe.

"What do you mean by clues, Joe?" asked Braxton, trying to understand Joe's rhyme and reason.

"OK. Well, again you're not going to believe me, but another set of clues comes in the form of crop circles!"

"Joe, they were debunked years ago!" Tina said.

"Look, I agree that there have been some made by pranksters. But I promise you this... for every prank there is a genuine crop circle. Some of them were too complex to build overnight, especially bearing in mind the crude methods the fraudsters used."

"OK, so can you show us one you think is genuine?" demanded Braxton.

"Sure," Joe opened a clip on his laptop that showed a response to the Voyager spacecraft interstellar radio message, sent in 1974. The message had been sent to globular star cluster M13, 25,000 light years away. The message could be decoded to represent our human race, in what was called the Arecibo Message. The crop circle was then dubbed the Arecibo Response, although in fact it was more of a crop rectangle. The crop response appeared in 2001, near the Chilbolton radio telescope in Hampshire, England. The imagery of the crop circle was without doubt incredibly complex. If this had been the work of jokers, they must have been exceptionally talented.

"It's hard to believe that this was done by a team of men overnight, Joe.

It's very impressive," admitted Braxton. "But how come we never see the aliens in action?"

How can proof be obtained on such a topic when the problem with today is that it's so easy to falsify imagery?

51. Alien Visitors and Abductions

Joe was on a roll. He had another theme he had just started researching – alien abductions.

Alien abductions are where one of a number of different types of events can occur. Typically, it's when an adult seemingly blacks out for a period of time, only to then find himself in another place not knowing how he got there, or why. Finally, flashbacks occur where the person remembers snippets of being abducted.

Another form of alien abduction is when people go missing, whether it be children or adults.

In the case of male adults being taken and returned, the general story is that they were seemingly examined, with sample tissues, DNA and perhaps even semen extracted.

The same was said for the females, who felt that they had not only been examined, but also used for fertility. It is suggested that eggs would have been stolen, and in some cases it was said that a few would give birth to a half human half alien hybrid, absurd and ludicrous as it may seem.

Joe started to explain how large numbers of children had gone missing over the millennia, typically orphaned children. Even back in Roman times, children were left abandoned by parents because they couldn't look after them. They were left in a place so that people were allowed to take them, people wishing for a family. Consequently children would disappear.

Joe seemed to run out of steam on this subject. It seemed he hadn't derived any conclusions about why these abductions were occurring, or where it might all be leading to. Perhaps it was because human eggs and semen were used elsewhere. Perhaps they were used in the alien world in order to continue their own race. Perhaps a half human half alien being would be re-sent to our own world. Either way, people do go missing, that's for sure. But there are of course many reasons why this might happen, usually very macabre reasons, sadly.

"You know, Joe, the human mind is a very powerful tool. Just look at some of the vivid dreams we have had ourselves. Days later, I swear sometimes I can't remember if they were real or just bad dreams." Tina tried to conjure an explanation for Joe's theory.

"That's true, Tina. I do wonder if it's possible to induce dreams by use of hints, words, imagery and sounds leading up to one's sleep. But the brain can also hide away bad experiences in order to protect itself from fear and destruction. Will we ever know?" concluded Joe.

52. Marathon Man

Dan and Mich proved to be quite a sporty couple. So much so that they even attempted a half marathon together. There was quite a lot of preparation involved in the months before the event. It meant that they were able to share their experiences throughout, including short runs in the morning and an ongoing diet for both of them that was ideal for their long distance running.

At first it was a struggle for them as they had to reprogram their mind-set. They had to set their alarm clocks at 6am, waking up to the winter darkness. Going out into the cold, dark, wet mornings was not very inviting at all. However, they soon established a routine. It no longer became a chore, it was actually quite refreshing. They even noticed their vastly improved alertness and attentiveness at their university lectures.

The best run came just after a large downfall of snow. As they met early in the morning there was a blanket of pure white snow, approximately five inches deep. It also layered across the tops of the trees. It was such a beautiful sight for Mother Nature to bestow. With the street lights casting brightness on the snow, and the dark shadows, the scene was truly romantic. On these mornings their run would end with a snowball fight and rolling on the ground, and they always made time to build a snowman – without a carrot nose.

Their worst mornings were those that followed, when the snow had melted with lashings of slush and ice on the ground. This caused lots of splashing and at times dangerous, slippery conditions. They always ended up exhausted but ultimately laughing with each other.

They always took a small flask of coffee, perhaps one of Mich's grand cafés, to drink at the end of their runs. Out of breath, they would reach the bottom steps of a large building and sit together sipping away at their beverages in anticipation of the sunrise. Occasionally Mich would take a large orange and peel it for the both of them, handing Dan a segment at a time.

They even enjoyed selecting their running outfits together, always ensuring the outfits either clashed or complemented each other. This often included hats and gloves in the winter, which they swapped occasionally.

It was a great experience for both of them, sharing special moments together.

Dan gained so much satisfaction and pleasure from the half marathon. He loved the adrenalin, so much so that he had decided to run a full marathon within the year.

Dan was always one for self-improvement and challenges. He would never contemplate running in fancy dress at marathons, for he took these events very seriously. He knew that on the day of the marathon there would be all sorts of individuals and clubs running for various charities. Runners would probably be dressed as animals or famous superheroes.

"Mich, I just can't imagine myself dressing up as a superhero or teddy bear! Imagine running with an extra layer of costume on top of my usual running kit! I seriously don't know how these guys do it when they are running as Batman or a furry animal." Mich laughed, imagining the scene, and gave Dan a cuddle.

People of all countries, nationalities and ages had run marathons for such a long time that each marathon had become very different from city to city. Some runners had even made it their profession, supplemented by sports sponsorships and advertising, and taking in all levels of commerce and business, including corporate events, lectures and team-building exercises.

Race times became quicker due to improved diets and a more professional level of training. The footwear became more hi-tech allowing less impact on the body's joints, especially when running on hard surfaces. But other than that it really hadn't changed much. It was a sport that had never changed over the centuries with the distance as always at 26.2 miles, or 42.195km.

In preparation, Dan decided to run a couple of half marathons leading up to the event and Mich joined him on the odd occasion. Together they had tremendous fun planning and preparing for the actual day, following their own diets and fitness routines.

They started a routine diet involving carbohydrates for the half marathons. Athletes were taught to sustain a regular regime prior to any event so that the body could maximise its energy levels. It almost became a science for both of them as Dan prepared for the full marathon.

Dan mostly trained during the winter and spring. Even the early summer had been a poor season for decent warm weather. Most of the time it was either cold or raining. But, as time crept closer to the day, in July, the weather was kind enough to provide some excellent balmy days. There was sun and heat to warm the body and soul.

Finally the moment arrived for the marathon, and the weather forecast predicted a scorcher with temperatures reaching a high of 34C. This was very unusual for an English summer. These days were rare, but enjoyed by all when they arrived.

The couple had not slept too well, either due to anxiety, excitement or simply race nerves. It had also been a rather hot evening, around the early 20s centigrade. Dan especially could not rest. He kept going through his strategy for the marathon. Should he start slow and gradually build his speed or should he sustain the same level of speed from beginning to end?

Dan and Mich were at the starting line early. There was plenty of time for him to find out where his starting position would be. Positions for each runner were determined by their previous experience. This allowed the authorities to assess each runner's ability within the group of runners.

Dan went through his warm-up routine. It involved numerous stretching exercises, kicking out his feet and flapping his arms by his side, performing lunges with his legs while resting his hands on the leading leg, a mid-air sprint and turning his head from side to side. Perhaps he didn't need to bother, for already the temperatures were in their mid-20s. Mich ordered Dan to drink as much water as possible. "You must, Dan! It's going to be a scorcher, and totally unbearable later. Make sure you do. OK?"

"Sure, sure, yes of course," replied Dan, as if to imply that he wasn't that stupid.

Mich and Dan embraced each other with excitement and sneaked a kiss. "Good luck, darling, see you at the end," said Mich lovingly.

Mich left Dan to continue his warm up, while she made her way to meet some friends near the finishing line, a few miles away on the other side of the city. They would await Dan's arrival a number of hours later.

As it was Dan's first full marathon, he found himself near the back of the competitors. He wasn't happy, especially as he was amongst a number of racers in fancy dress including an ostrich, a gorilla and several ducks. He did wonder if the ducks were part of a running club as there must have been around seven of them, all identical in various heights. He could even hear them quacking at each other in jest, which made him chuckle to himself. He found it quite funny and thought how silly.

There must have been over 1,000 people competing and he was amongst the ones doing it for fun. But really he wanted to take the event seriously and set a personal best that would impress his friends and family. He would show them!

Dan was confident because he felt that his half marathons in preparation of this race had gone well. He knew his times were better than average and he also knew he could push himself even harder.

From the offset Dan was keen to advance forward and pass as many runners as possible. Perhaps this was not the best way to start a marathon, as one is taught to pace oneself and build strength and heart rate as the race progresses, but Dan wanted to be among the serious racers.

He was amazed at the number of people in the crowd. He just couldn't believe how popular these occasions had become. The crowds were mostly in groups, all cheering on their friends as well as strangers. The buzz and energy was infectious, spurring the runners on to greater momentum. The crowd carried flags and banners, all with names and club logos, in different shapes, colours and sizes. The occasional hooter or fog horn went off to add to the cacophony of cheers.

Along the way there were several points at which the runners could take cups of water to rehydrate, but in Dan's determination to catch up with the leader group he had run past them without stopping, though he knew that at some opportunity soon he should.

At one point he hit a pain barrier, slowing down due to stitch, holding the left side of his ribcage, and trying hard to regain his second wind. He knew it was just a question of time before this would pass. A couple of ducks overtook him, squawking quack quack as they passed by, which he found a little embarrassing. After a while the stitch slowly disappeared, and again Dan found himself wanting to make up the time and overtake as many runners as he could – including the ducks! When he did pass them, it gave Dan great pleasure in quacking back at them! Perhaps his competitive streak made him his own worst enemy.

After 21 miles, Dan found himself feeling dizzy and unable to focus. He saw the road inch closer to him and he blacked out. He collapsed, falling to the ground and hitting the road hard. Assistants at the roadside made their way through the flow of competitors to Dan. They phoned through to their HQ to alert medics who arrived within minutes in an ambulance. Meanwhile, the runners continued passing by, focused on their task ahead.

Dan was stretchered into an ambulance and driven to the A&E department at the local hospital. In the ambulance the medics fought desperately to revive him. He had gone into a cardiac arrest.

Meanwhile Mich was standing close to the finish line, waiting patiently for her hero to arrive. She had no knowledge of the events that had just unfolded five miles away.

Sadly, Dan died in the ambulance before reaching the hospital. The medics had failed to revive him.

53. At The Finish

Dan's body was kept at the hospital. As she was the love of his life, he had given Mich's contact details as the next of kin on the application form for the marathon.

Mich stood in excitement by the road with her friend Henri keeping her company. They continued to watch the clock, wondering when Dan would pass by. They really had no idea when he would arrive because it was his first marathon. Together with Henri, Mich had a great time watching the passing parade. There had in fact already been three Batmans, two Robins and two Supermans. No ducks, but they had seen an ostrich. All very funny, all waving as they passed by. Mich and Henri shared a mini picnic which included a flask of coffee along with some cheese and lettuce sandwiches. At times they squatted on the floor to give their legs a rest. Every now and again they would stand to see who else would be running by in disguise. But still no sight of Dan.

Mich's phone rang. It was the police calling about Dan. They offered their condolences and told Mich where Dan's body was. They needed her to identify the body. Mich collapsed, Henri looked on and caught her as she tumbled in shock.

Henri, along with several bystanders, helped Mich to regain control and someone handed her a cup of water. She was able to stand up but felt very weak. She was stuttering and wanted Henri to call her father. She needed him. Henri called him and they agreed to meet at the exit to the marathon boundary. He would be waiting in the car.

Mich was struggling to walk or talk. She just sobbed and kept shaking her head. Her world had caved in. She just couldn't think straight. As much as Henri tried to comfort her, Mich heard nothing. She just kept thinking of Dan, her poor Dan.

Mich's father drove as fast as he could and all together they went to the accident and emergency department at the local hospital. While Henri comforted Mich, her father went into the reception area. They were asked to wait. Mich just kept sobbing and looking at the floor, not wanting to raise her head, as if she was curling up deep inside.

Mich's father realised Dan's fathers needed to be informed. Where would he start? How could he console them over the phone?

He left Henri and Mich for a moment. He exited the room and found a quiet area to phone Dan's fathers. He gave the address of the hospital but knew that it would take a couple of hours before they would arrive.

Mich's mind worked overtime thinking about what could have been done prior to the event. If he hadn't taken part in this marathon Dan would still be alive. Her mind flashed back to all the times they had together, from the moment they met, to the last kiss before the marathon.

Maybe time would heal, but right now time was standing still. Mich didn't want to live any more. She wanted to be with Dan.

She was a child again, playing in a park.

She was an even younger child wanting to cuddle someone, being told she couldn't, it wasn't allowed.

She didn't want to live any more.

Mich's father decided that the trauma was too much for her. He tried to explain to her that she could visit Dan when she was ready – maybe later, maybe the following day. Her father also thought that maybe she needed some form of medication to help her calm down. He spoke with a doctor who gave her a sedative and suggested she should rest at home.

Mich's father went into the room where Dan lay and it was he who identified the body. He spoke with the staff, informing them that Dan's fathers would arrive shortly.

He felt that this was all he could do for the moment and so he took Mich and Henri home as Mich drifted into a sleep.

54. Fathers United

The next day all three fathers agreed to meet at the hospital in order to be at Mich's side when it came to her time to see Dan. How hard this must be for someone so young.

Henri, along with her partner Bobbi, had also agreed to come along to support Mich. They were good friends to Mich in her time of need.

The three fathers got together to organise the next steps to lay Dan to rest.

They agreed to speak again over the phone, and that Mich's father would organise everything – for there was a known procedure to follow, especially for Dan.

55. Extrapolation

Joe arrived at Braxton and Tina's in the early evening. He had been invited to stay over and keep Braxton company while Tina was away for the weekend, visiting her parents in the north of England.

Both Joe and Braxton enjoyed these get-togethers every couple of months. It was a real brotherly bonding experience, infused religiously with copious amounts of beer. As always, towards the end of the evening, they would move on to either whiskey or Cognac. By the end of these evenings, both of them would be so far gone that Joe would stay over in the spare bedroom. They even kept some of Joe's spare clothes and pyjamas in one of the wardrobes, along with a toothbrush.

They typically brought out the old chess set from one of the cabinets in the lounge, for a head to head combat. The set had been bought from a stall at a local craft market many years before, during Braxton's latter teenage years. It was made of a type of wax resin and carved with a Greek theme, with the god Apollo as the king together with the goddess Hera as the queen.

They had forgotten who had won the most games, although Joe believed it to be himself, even if he had lost count. As they sat and contemplated their next moves they would discuss the world, their theories and their opinions.

Most often, although perhaps he knew he shouldn't, Braxton would confide in Joe about some of his crime cases. It did no harm to hear a layman's point of view. Perhaps it would give him another angle to consider, in order to solve the mystery, even if it was Joe and his wild theories.

Tonight was no exception, although Braxton was even more cautious as he explained the two mysterious bodies discovered in the cemetery. As Braxton described what he had seen Joe was completely enthralled, his mind working away to solve the riddle. In many ways Joe and Braxton were much alike, perhaps they had inherited this quality from their father who would often play the game of chess whenever the family came together for festive reunions.

"A game of chess is excellent exercise for the brain, one can formulate ideas and plan future moves or decisions in life," their father would sagely surmise.

Joe started the game, launching one of his pawns forward into battle in a confident manner. As usual there was the standard set of chess moves that kept the pair of them occupied until the game became more complex and slowed down. At this stage each move required more thought and process. It also gave them more time to think through their thoughts and opinions on possible explanations for the two bodies.

There was a number of key factors about the two dead bodies that Braxton and Joe considered.

One: The bodies were both really tall, over 7ft tall in fact. This was rare. If we think of the average height of a man and woman at the beginning of the 21st Century, then these were not your average people. Maybe they were Dutch?

Two: They were tested as being very old. Yet, on appearance they looked young. This was strange and must surely have been an error in the biopsy. But what if it were true?

Three: They were bald and completely hairless.

Joe and Braxton were dumbfounded. Although there were conditions that made this plausible, for both of them to be like that was very strange.

Four: Their genitalia were either missing or very small in proportion to their height. Again Joe and Braxton were at a loss due to their lack of medical knowledge.

"You know, Joe, I did some research and found that the average height of the Dutch increased by 20 cm, or eight inches, over a 150-year period. This means that in another 150 years, their average height will be over two metres –that's over 7ft tall! Weirdly, they were gauged to be around that age, around 150 years old! Isn't that incredible? A real coincidence!" Braxton was trying to start a thread of logic.

"I don't believe in coincidences, Braxton, and I know you don't either. Even you said that they don't look from this world! I mean, who normally fits that profile?"

There was a pause as both surveyed the chess board. Joe made another move, with Braxton nodding his head in acknowledgement of a correct tactic.

"OK, Joe, let's go mad! Let's go in to your world - the world of Joe. If this was on your internet search with your internet theories, what would you say is going on?"

"Seriously?!" said Joe, who gave it a little thought as Braxton made his move. "Then I would say they came from either another world similar to ours, or from another time. Like let's say from 150 years into our future. Certainly we can extrapolate that from the Dutch guys."

"Yeah, I thought you might say that! Great! So I go to my boss and tell him they are from the future!" Braxton looked Joe in the eye, and they both burst out laughing as they gulped down more beer.

"But.... also..... you forget very easily don't you Braxton?" said Joe

"What do you mean, Joe?"

"I can't help remembering that experience you had when you were back in college. Even to this day I feel that your strange encounter fuelled my love of conspiracies"

"Oh right, you mean those two tall guys in black sitting on a bench in Hyde Park? Well as I told you at the time Joe, I think I had dreamt it, simply because the whole episode was very surreal" said Braxton.

"Sure, but from what I remember you saying at the time, doesn't their description kind of seem similar to the dead couple? Also you said their ages were way off the scale" added Joe.

"Well, I have to admit Joe, I still question myself about all of that. The whole incident passed by for such a short instance, I'd wished I had recorded it to believe it."

A couple of seconds of silence and reflection followed.

"Maybe there really are people who visit from the future" stated Braxton with his eyes open wide, as if looking into space.

Both brothers held that thought.

"Check!" stated Braxton, who seemed to realise his discussion with Joe meant he had an advantage over him, as Joe was preoccupied with trying to unravel this mystery of the two dead bodies.

"Oh, wait!" Joe gave some thought and moved a piece to intercept the attack from Braxton's piece. He quickly returned to the case in question.

"I suppose I would be asking, why dig a grave there? I mean why there and not some other place? Did you ask that question, Braxton?"

"Yes, of course, it was one of the first questions we asked ourselves, as well as motives, etc. At the moment, we don't even know how one of them died. Our doctor is still baffled. It's a complete mystery!

"But you're right, Joe. If only we could at least understand why they were buried in this cemetery, and why there particularly. Why would they not go through official channels for the burial? That's what makes it even more suspicious. Usually, if there's a murder, then they dump the bodies in a forest or lake, somewhere remote, but this was like a formal burial."

Another pause and Braxton made a move. "Checkmate!" exclaimed Braxton, and saluted with his right fist into the air. "Your turn to get the beers, Joe!"

"D'oh! You had me distracted," said Joe. "That's cheating! Set them up again, I demand a re-match!" Joe stormed off into the kitchen to fetch two more beers.

56. Father's Dilemma

During the night, Mich's head was pounding from a severe migraine. Her mind shifted constantly. She slept most of the time, but kept reliving the events of the marathon day. Then came flashbacks from her childhood days. She was completely caught up between the two moments of her life, and between the two, she didn't want to be anywhere. She no longer knew who she was nor where she belonged.

The next morning she ate breakfast with her father, but left most of it on her plate, sipping only a little of her coffee. Her head hung towards the floor and her mind was all over the place as she fidgeted constantly at the table. Then without warning she confronted her father.

"Who am I, Father?" she demanded bluntly.

"What do you mean, Mich?"

"Do I have a mother? Where is she? I don't have my Dan, I don't have a mother."

"Mich, you have me. I'm sorry that we can't bring Dan back. It will take time. It's not helping now I know, but we must fight through this. I will help you."

"I don't know who I am or where I come from. I feel helpless. I just don't want to live. I want to be with Dan. Let me die with him. I don't belong here." She was almost in a locked place. Like a very young child, afraid with nowhere to go. Her constant torment fatigued her, and even though it was only approaching mid-day she soon returned to her bedroom exhausted. She closed the blinds and drifted back to sleep, in order to escape.

As the dark wrapped around Mich, her father pondered how he could help her in her time of need. He knew he would have to help her understand who she was. Even worse, he would also have to explain who poor Dan was.

57. The Time of Truth

What could Mich's father say to his daughter?

It was always only ever going to be a matter of time before she would want to know the truth about her origins. Or should he hold back? Wouldn't it be in her interest to try to help her move forward and get on with her life?

He himself couldn't think of anyone to turn to for counsel. He was a wise and spiritual man who had lived for a great number of years. Yet, even with such knowledge and experience, he still felt inadequate.

"Is my mother a surrogate?" demanded Mich.

"No Mich, she is not."

"But you are my father aren't you?" Mich looked him straight in the eye, waiting for a reaction.

Mich's father turned away from her, looking down at the floor, trying to think how he could express himself.

"Why don't you tell me the truth?" Mich was becoming almost hysterical.

"You're holding something back from me! I deserve to know, I deserve to!" Mich was starting to lose control again.

"OK, Mich, calm down! This is very hard to explain, and I am not sure you will understand… You have some of my genes in you, and so there is a part of me in you."

"So you are my father… So who is my mother?"

"Well it's not as simple as that because normally with single parents there is either a surrogate mother, or adoption…" explained her father, but before he could finish she reacted again.

"So I have no surrogate mother, but there is a part of you in me, but I'm not adopted? These are riddles! Stop hurting me with this nonsense!" cried Mich.

"I'm sorry, I'm trying hard not to do that. You are correct… you're neither," replied her father.

"Then… oh no! Oh, my! Are you telling me… I'm a clone? But wouldn't I be a male if I had some of you?" Mich seemed to despair. She almost wanted to collapse on the floor, as her energy depleted. She wished she hadn't asked, but she needed to know. It was all too unreal.

"Mich, you are a beautiful, intelligent young woman. I am so proud of you. Does it matter what you are? You have a part of me inside you, and you are an individual with wants and needs like anyone else in this world." Her father tried so hard to make her realise that she was an individual with all the qualities of every other person, and more.

"No! I won't accept this! You should tell me now! What the hell am I?"

"OK… You are a biological robot. It is similar to a clone, but built to a specified program of genes and chromosomes, that also includes some of my genes and chromosomes. There is no mother, only a place where you developed into a beautiful child. There I've said it," concluded her father.

Mich said nothing. She was speechless. It was as if she had been punched. How does a person respond to that? She stormed off and slammed her bedroom door shut, climbed in to her bed and cried the rest of the day and night, until she fell asleep.

58. Of Another Time

The next morning, Mich rose and went through the motions with her father, preparing and eating breakfast. She ate all of hers, and even polished off three coffees. After anger came disbelief, perhaps this was just a very bizarre tale. It was no good attacking her father. It wasn't his fault, and in fact he was her only source of strength at this critical crisis.

This time she was calm as she spoke: "Father, I looked on the internet this morning to find that there is no such thing as a biological robot – it doesn't exist. The only reference was from a scientist who had a weird idea, but it was rejected as some bizarre theory. So... are you just trying to protect me? I will accept what I am. I understand I feel and act the same as anyone else, so I can't believe I'm an alien. So what am I, Father? Come on... tell me... please." Mich could not have spoken more calmly to her father. He was taken aback at how relaxed she seemed, after all she had gone through.

"OK. You should know that you are as much a human being as I am. You are my daughter... even if you weren't my biological daughter, I have loved you since you were born, since you came into my life, please understand that! OK?" stated her father.

"The reason why you haven't heard of a biological robot is because it is technology from an advanced time. In essence, it is during this future that you were born into the world.

"But… why are you here in this time, you might be asking? Well, it's because there is a part in you that has feelings… heterosexual feelings that in the future are suppressed and forbidden. I couldn't see you develop in such a society, so I brought you here to blossom into a beautiful and loving woman. An adoring flower who one day would be able to express her love for someone." Mich's father was holding back his tears.

"The way in which the biological robot is made is no different to any other natural process. The genes and chromosomes are mixed together from the two partners through a pseudo natural conception. The only difference is that I was able to choose my genes along with a random selection of other genes. They were all effectively from a pool of better quality genes.

"Your biological make-up is such that you should not suffer from any diseases or ailments. This is because the genes that cause these are not in you, as they are in others who may suffer later in life.

"The reason why this is done in the future is because Man had moved to an asexual society. Humanity had already started to lose the ability to procreate due to the way society was changing, and so they worked with IVF. But, the process then started rejecting the embryos and very soon they turned towards cloning.

"The quality of the gene pool is so essential to the quality of a species, but unfortunately, after a while, the gene pool became less and less. There had to be a way to increase it in order to save the human race. So they realised that they should attempt and mimic the natural process by mixing up the genes and chromosomes. Eventually, they could select which ones they wanted and which could be randomly generated. This increased the gene pool and allowed natural parentage where possible. The main aim was to recreate a society where procreation would become natural again, with the hope that there would be no need for any scientific help in the future.

"At one time, the only way to increase the gene pool was to bring babies from a past epoch into our society. The babies were from a period where heterosexuality was still strong, where the gene pool was good, so they were brought into the future as a way to procreate. But they didn't expect such a strong asexual society, and so biological robots are now a part of future society. Perhaps one day Man will return to natural procreation." Mich's father ran out of breath.

"Are you saying you took babies from another period in time, and brought them into the future in order to increase the gene pool? That's disgraceful! What about the parents of these babies?" asked Mich.

"Yes I agree, but at the time the future of the humanity was at breaking point. There was a period where they felt there was a real chance that the human race could become extinct because the whole procreation of Man was failing. They were desperate measures, Mich, we all regret these actions."

"You said 'we'. Are you saying you were a part of this?" Mich couldn't believe her ears.

"It was part of my job to research methods to increase the gene pool at that time, whilst we looked for a more ethical solution. We had to take these babies in order to sustain a balance of life. We always tried to take orphans, or rejected babies, and we tried so hard not to break up families," explained her father.

"As an example, like many other societies the Romans would abandon their infants. This was generally known as exposure because the infants were exposed to the elements. Exposure was also used on children whose paternity was unclear or undesirable. But not all infants who were exposed died. Some of the Roman infants were picked up by other families for slavery. But some of the children were saved, not just from slavery, but from death." Her father was trying to justify their actions.

"However, there were the odd accidental exceptions that were regrettable… which comes to my confession to you." Mich's father had come all this way and now he realised he could not hold back. It was only fair to Mich and he hoped Mich would forgive him.

"What is it, Father?"

Mich's father could hardly speak. His mouth was dry and he felt a lump in his throat as he tried to explain. He took his time and breathed slowly to calm himself... "Dan was taken as a baby from this past. He was a child from the 19th Century. A time when the gene pool had already started to weaken, but still a time of some strength." ... There... it was said. But Mich's father was still not sure at all if he should have said it. His eyes looked down, he was afraid of how this would affect Mich.

Mich was silent. There was so much to understand and believe – that this was not just a crazy story. She knew her father could not make this up, nor would he, for he loved her dearly. But it was too unreal. He would not want to hurt her and at the same time she trusted him.

Mich's father returned his gaze to Mich, to demonstrate his sincerity.

"When we go to Dan's funeral, we shall take him back to his time. We shall place him with his family, in order to reunite them," said Mich's father. He was trying to resolve his guilt. But at the same time, this method of returning those that were taken from the past was an agreed legal policy within his group of peers.

"This is just not real, Father," said Mich. "It's just not real. It's surreal! This is not a time to joke!"

"I'm sorry, Mich, but what I am telling you here, you have to believe is the truth. We will take Dan back to his time and we will bury him with his family," concluded her father.

Mich was in total disbelief. She decided to go outside and take a walk in the fresh air. At the end of the road was the park that she remembered from her childhood. She opened the gate, went into the park and sat on a bench overlooking the playground, with its roundabout and swings. Nothing much had changed since her childhood. It still gave her a warm feeling inside. But she knew there was a time prior to this when she had been unhappy. She couldn't explain it. She tried hard to go further back in her memory. There were a couple of children playing close by, their squeals of fun were amusing and again gave Mich some flashbacks to her long distant memories. "Oh, what fun we had," she thought to herself.

As her mind drifted further, she remembered trying to kiss a boy, how he refused and screamed whilst a teacher scolded her. She now remembered how her father was asked to take her out of school. It was now very clear. Was this what her father was trying to explain?

And then her mind drifted back to Dan. She was lost, and again she felt no strength, no understanding of what she wanted to do other than to be with Dan.

59. Further Investigations

Detective Constable Braxton perched at his desk, contemplating the next move in his investigation. He shared an office with a number of fellow constables, whilst Detective Sergeant Dawson's office was close by. DC Waites was stationed at the next desk to Braxton. She was a relatively young and new recruit to CID, and Braxton could see that she looked up to both Dawson and himself with respect.

Braxton sat and pondered for a while as he sipped his piping hot coffee, fresh from the vending machine. He looked out of the window for inspiration. "It's raining again," he said to Waites, who comically acknowledged the obvious statement, raising her eyes to the ceiling and giving a little shrug of her shoulders.

"Great. So I go to Dawson and I tell him they are from the future... or from another planet." That thought had stuck in Braxton's head since the chess night with Joe. He couldn't let it go. It's crazy!

He looked around at Waites and his other colleagues. He thought that not only would they laugh at him, but they would also consider him slightly mad. What kind of role model would he be for Waites? Since when did they do aliens from another planet in training? He chuckled to himself.

He had not slept since his evening with Joe and his conspiracy theories. Joe may be his younger, wacky brother, but he knew that he was an incredibly bright spark, and that somewhere in his madness there may be a hint of truth in all that he theorised. He had also reflected on his weird encounter of the two extremely tall men in black in Hyde Park… were they just an illusion or should he read more into this … message.

Braxton's training within the police force gave him an even more logical brain than before. He knew he had to work on facts and figures, evidence and proof, even motive. But Joe gave him that something else, another dimension of lateral logic, of thinking outside the box. Perhaps he should take what Joe said, and work it into his own framework. This would then allow Braxton to share his own thoughts with his boss DS Dawson in a professional manner.

Braxton felt that there was still more to understand about this unusual couple, even if it did feel like he had hit a brick wall.

The buried couple were naked, cocooned in some unusual material – so what was that made of? It didn't look like any material he had seen before, although it did remind him of a material similar to a spider's web, and the stuff used to wrap baggage at airports. He could ask forensics to find out where that cocoon webbing might have come from. And as Joe had questioned – why in that cemetery? It couldn't have been random, could it? And why in that particular location? Is there a link somewhere?

Braxton gave a call to his colleague Johnson in forensics in order to arrange an analysis of the cocoon material. He then phoned Mike at the cemetery to say he would visit again that afternoon.

"We'll have some tea ready for when you arrive, and I expect Joyce will have something baked to go with it," said Mike.

60. Cemetery Revisited

Most days Braxton would work through his lunch hour, grabbing a sandwich and eating it at his desk. But he realised it wasn't a healthy habit, so more recently he had been trying to venture out for lunch as often as he could. He would typically arrange to meet Tina at some nearby diner or bistro. It gave him a break from the stresses of work and his struggles to solve cases. But more importantly, it also gave him a chance to see more of Tina. It also gave Tina the chance to monitor Braxton's new diet.

One day, after a salad lunch with Tina, Braxton drove over to the cemetery to meet Mike Stevens and his team.

He was greeted by Mike and invited into the office where Joyce and Colin were sitting at the main table. Braxton could immediately see that they had prepared a cup of tea and scones for his arrival. "We thought you might like a cup of tea and some of Joyce's home-made scones, her speciality," Mike said with a grin on his face.

"Wow! That's great. Many thanks. I won't say no. That's very kind of you," thanked Braxton.

Mike poured the tea as Joyce set out the plates. A larger plate was placed in the centre of the table, piled high with strawberry jam-filled scones, "Stretch your hand, don't be afraid to take one, young man," said Joyce in a motherly sort of way.

"Thanks, Joyce, they look delicious," replied Braxton, and promptly took his scone.

"So, what can we do for you, Detective?" asked Mike.

"Well, we need to find more evidence on this case," Braxton replied. "As you know it's a very unusual situation here. I can't imagine you would have had this happen before, have you?"

"You can say that again! Even our regional office is curious to see what happens. This is highly unusual and very bizarre," said Mike.

"I can imagine. So what we want to know is a bit more about this cemetery. Do you know how long it's been a cemetery? Is there any logic in the way the grounds are structured? I mean, as an example, was the original cemetery on smaller grounds? Were the grounds expanded? Are there areas for specific types of burials? I'm really fishing here, but hope you can give me some understanding of how the place is set up," said Braxton, really hoping something would come from this information.

"Sure, Detective, we can help you with that. Let's see, where should we start?" Mike asked himself as he looked at Joyce and Colin for support. "OK, so let's look at the layout and the history of the cemetery.

"Well, as you may know, the cemetery was formed on a hill. There are 44 acres of land. Two spacious and elegant chapels were erected with a gateway in between, over which is a tower with a stone staircase. At the top of the tower there are charming and far-reaching views. There are two lodges. The grounds have been planted and laid out with paths in an attractive manner." Mike was beginning to sound like a real estate agent.

"The cemetery was built in advance of actual requirements, so is immense compared to the number of graves over time. It has seats for people who have climbed the hill, and have a desire to rest. They are also able to take tea, and maybe some scones..." Mike smiled at Braxton, "... at the second lodge." Braxton took a bite of his scone.

"The hill is in fact the highest point in the parish. It's over 200ft above sea level. The lowest point in the parish being 60ft above sea level. The hill now has the most charming view of the surrounding district, which of course is much extended from the top of the tower.

"A number of cannon balls were found at the beginning of the 1800s in a field on the western side of the hill. This is now forming part of the cemetery. Workmen were ploughing there, and interestingly enough our old retired groundsman Mr Beecham's grandfather was one of them and was there when the ploughshare turned up the balls.

"The location where the balls were found fits very well with the description given of the temporary lodging-place of the King's troops. But the date of that event appears too early for the age of the balls, which were further examined by experts. They were of the opinion that their date was Cromwellian, the date of the Civil War, possibly about 1643.

"It is reported that one of our very old retired churchwardens said that when he was a boy, old labourers in a nearby village pointed out the spot where, in the Civil War, Oliver Cromwell placed his cannon on the hill to fire at the local castle. That spot was measured as being in the cemetery.

"So you see there has been quite some history here relating to the English Civil War.

"As to the original grounds, the majority of the earliest graves are to the rear of our main buildings, including the church. The oldest grave dates back to 1723, although we think there may be graves even older, due to the Civil War. The war lasted between 1642 and 1651. But the earliest marked grave is, as I said, 1723.

"As more graves were dug, they were dug concentrically outwards from the main buildings. There are some exceptions, for example where families are able to reserve spaces for future generations.

"The graves of today are down at the bottom of the hill to the east side, you can tell simply by the style of the gravestones." Mike stopped to see if he needed to go on, waiting for Braxton to respond.

"Thanks, Mike. So the area where our new grave was found, you would say is more in the area where the old original graves were?" asked Braxton.

"Not the earliest graves, Detective, but certainly ones that were perhaps around the 200-year mark, maybe less."

"And you don't dig graves there any more?" quizzed Braxton.

"Oh no. In a way, those areas are protected and consequently we don't ever dig new graves there. Any reservation of graves is further away, way down the hill around the more recent graves… well, when I say recent, I mean within this last century," replied Mike.

"Thanks, Mike. You've been really helpful, I appreciate your time today. I actually have my grandparents buried here, so I might go and pay my respects to them now," concluded Braxton, and he thanked the team for the tea and scones.

What with the bistro lunches, and the visits to the cemetery with tea and cakes or scones, Braxton was starting to put on a bit of weight.

Braxton left the office and turned to his left to walk down the winding gravel path, in search of his grandparents' grave. The air was fresh and clean and he was glad he had worn a scarf and heavy coat. As he walked down the path he could hear the steady crunching of the gravel underneath his shoes with no other sound around him. He reflected on the tranquility of the grounds and how Mike and his team had kept them in good condition.

He reached his grandparents' grave after making a few detours. He remembered how in his previous visits he had never managed to find the grave the first time. However, his memory would soon become familiar with the surrounding gravestones as he narrowed down his search. The cemetery always felt like a labyrinth. But now he stood overlooking his grandparents' modest grave.

Braxton had loved his grandparents. They had always been devoted to him and his siblings. He was the eldest grandchild and felt nothing but love and kindness from them. He stood and reflected on his time with them, and on his childhood.

Often his mother would drop him off at his grandparents' house after school on the Friday and he would stay with them for the whole weekend. It was during this time he bonded most with his grandfather who would teach and encourage him with mathematics and who would often play word games with him. In some ways, this time with his grandparents almost made Braxton feel like an only child, receiving full attention while at the same time being allowed to be creative in amusing himself.

Isn't it incredible how time flies? The clock is always ticking. One minute we are surrounded by our nearest and dearest, but then they are gone.

He was only 10 years old when he lost his grandfather. He had been a heavy smoker all his life, dying at the premature age of 60 after suffering for a number of months. Braxton remembered how he had wept over the loss of his grandfather for weeks, and from that day forward he had an intrinsic hatred for smoking – not only was it a smelly filthy habit but more importantly... a killer. He missed that special bond with his grandfather, and even today it had left a huge gap in his life.

His grandmother had done remarkably well on her own and lived to her 80s. She was adorable, and again Braxton missed her very much.

"I miss you both," Braxton whispered to them as he turned to go home. He sauntered over to his car, reflecting on what he had been told by Mike, but nothing really seemed to be evident. Perhaps something would hit him during his sleep, as it often did.

Braxton got into his car and drove home for the evening.

61. Webbing

The next day Braxton went over to see Johnson at forensics to follow up on the analysis of the cocoon's wrapping material.

The pair of them wondered if they had discovered a modern day Egyptian style mummy because, as is common knowledge, these mummies were wrapped in cloth. But perhaps that was where the similarities ended, because one observation was clear, and that was that the famous Egyptian mummies were all shrivelled up with their brains literally pulled out of their heads, whereas this couple was in an almost perfect condition.

Johnson started by saying that he was aware of new materials being manufactured that were on the edge of technology. "This webbing cloth around the bodies is not your everyday cotton or polyester, Braxton," he said.

"The webbing is very much of a polymer material that we are not aware of. Although I do know there are scientists from Hokkaido University and Tokai University in Japan developing a nanosheet. It's made of a fluorine-containing polymer for use in wrapping biological samples. The nanosheet retains high water repellent properties and helps to retain a sample's water content when used as a wrapper.

"Although my understanding is that this material is still at an early stage. It could be years before we see it," said Johnson.

"If it's something like this, then that could explain why the bodies are still in exceptional condition," he concluded.

"So, Johnson, what you are saying is you don't recognise the material?" summarised Braxton.

"Sorry, but in essence, yes. This is something you don't buy in shops or on the internet. In fact I don't believe we have anything like it today, other than, as I say, what's going on in Japan, and that's not going to be available for quite some years," concluded Johnson.

Both stared into space for a moment to contemplate.

"Thanks, Johnson, much appreciated. Please keep looking. Let me know if you come up with anything else." Braxton returned to the office.

Back at his desk and with a cup of hot tea in his hand, Braxton decided to research Egyptian mummies.

62. Egyptian Mummies

Braxton was browsing the internet for information about Egyptian mummies, especially the process of mummification.

Ancient Egyptians believed in the afterlife when someone died, and mummification was seen as a way to help someone reach it. The Egyptians thought that in order to have an afterlife, the dead person would have to repossess his or her body. They believed that the only way to do this was if the body was recognisable.

The chief embalmer was a priest closely associated with mummification and embalming.

This is the step-by-step process of how mummification took place:

1. Insert a hook through a hole near the nose and pull out part of the brain
2. Make a cut on the left side of the body near the stomach
3. Remove all internal organs
4. Let the internal organs dry
5. Place the lungs, intestines, stomach and liver inside canopic jars
6. Place the heart back inside the body
7. Rinse the inside of the body with wine and spices
8. Cover the corpse with salt for 70 days

9. After 40 days, stuff the body with linen or sand to give it a more human shape
10. After the 70 days, wrap the body from head to toe in bandages
11. Place in a sarcophagus, which is a type of coffin

Braxton mumbled under his breath. "And simmer for 30 mins before raising to the boil," as any food recipe would request.

He sat back and concluded: "Well that was a waste of time! The only thing in common here is the wrapping of the body in bandages, and perhaps seeking a way to keep their bodies intact for their afterlife. Our two bodies were completely intact and had hardly aged.

"Nope, our couple were not mummies, that's for sure," Braxton thought aloud. "Unless they, whoever they are, have upgraded their techniques."

63. Body Preservation

Braxton decided to give George a quick call to arrange a meeting as he was curious as to how a dead body could still look in such excellent condition after death.

Immediately after the call he popped into his car and sped over to her lab.

"So, you want to know what happens to a body after death?" repeated George.

"Well at least some understanding of it, please. It's just that they looked so fresh, if fresh is the right term. I still can't believe that they seem to be in such perfect condition," stated Braxton.

"Yes, I know what you mean, Braxton. I have to say I think the cloth used to cocoon the bodies may have helped, because since the cloth has been removed, I can now see some decomposition. Mind you, it's still only minor. As you know, the labs and cold chambers here are very cold for a reason!

"The wives' tale is that bodies these days don't decay as quickly as they did years ago. As you may already know, life expectancy has increased too. Some say that it's partly down to what we eat." George looked at Braxton for a reaction, and she got one as Braxton raised his eyebrows, somewhat surprised.

"Yes, I thought that might surprise you, but if you think about it, it kind of makes sense," continued George.

"The amount of additives and preservatives, or E numbers, added to food has meant that our bodies absorb these chemicals into our digestive system. In essence, the theory was that our skin and organs contain a preservation chemical that makes them last longer, giving us a longer life expectancy... and, as it also seems... preserving the organs after death.

"The role of preservatives in our foods is to stop the processes of oxidation and bacterial growth. You might be thinking that this is a good thing, and it is, depending on which types of preservatives are being used.

"Preservatives can be placed into two different categories – natural and man-made.

"There are many different types of natural preservatives. Acids, like citrus juice for example, prevent the oxidation of food. Salt is another one which has been used for thousands of years. Oils and vinegars are also commonly used to preserve food. These natural substances only attack the bad bacteria and encourage good bacteria.

"In contrast, man-made preservatives are not great because they attack both good and bad bacteria. We need the good bacteria to help our bodies digest.

"However, returning to the other part about body decomposition after death – you know… there is actually no scientific reason why preservatives should prolong after-death body decomposition. The reason is because these preservatives, after entering our system, are broken down and dissolved or excreted away. So, I am at a loss as to why our two are in such good condition. I can only think that it's down to their genetic makeup… that they have healthier genes.

"This couple do seem to be taking longer to decompose than normal, which is a little startling. But, as I have said, we are now slowly seeing the effects, although it appears as if the male has more advanced decomposition than the female," concluded George.

"Thanks, George. That's interesting, but I am not sure I have anything to go on. Let me know if anything else develops, please." Braxton yet again felt like he had reached another dead end.

64. Night's Sleep

It was late evening, and as usual Braxton and Tina were in bed and chatting about their day or life in general. Typically when they were not chatting they each had a book in their hand to read.

Braxton told Tina how he had revisited the cemetery and had also seen his grandparents' grave. He explained how he had found it quite spiritual and satisfying, reminiscing about the times with them. Tina sat listening with empathy and a smile on her face, happy to share these private moments with her love.

"You didn't tell me about your grandparents being buried there," Tina said. "Why didn't you say so?"

"I would have loved to have come with you to pay my respects. Maybe next time I can come along?" asked Tina.

"Sure, yes of course. I wouldn't have thought it would have been of interest. But yes, I'd like that!" replied Braxton.

Braxton reflected on his recent visit. Somehow it seems to be human nature to return to your ancestry, a certain pulling towards your kindred spirit. Could this be why the two dead bodies were buried in this specific cemetery?

65. Switching Off

That night, before Mich went to bed, she spoke to her father in such a way that he knew there was no turning back for his daughter. She was too determined and focused on being with Dan.

"Father, if as you say I am a biological robot, then is it possible to switch me off? Is there a mechanism that does this in a humane way?" she asked calmly.

"This is an extreme measure, Mich. You are grieving and perhaps you are not thinking rationally. I would not be your father if I were to let you just give up. You have still so much to give and cherish in your precious life."

"I have given this much thought, and I know it's what I want. I want to be with Dan! Please, Father." Mich would not relent.

Mich's father was of another time, a time which had seen the progression of euthanasia based on compassion for those who were suffering. He would need to approach his peers for counsel. He felt that he needed their opinions on whether he was doing the right thing.

Scientists had previously inserted a mechanism into biological robots as a precaution should a problem arise with the robot's development. In the beginning robots were almost experimental and at times a danger to themselves more than anyone. But then there came a time when their development had been refined and proven to be safe, perhaps with the odd exception. However, the switch was kept as a safeguard.

The switch was in fact under and at the rear of the cranium in the external acoustic meatus, close to the mastoid part of the temporal bone. To turn off the robot, there was a special sonic device that would fire a sound of 70kHz at the switch for 10 seconds. This would close down the robot's biological system, very similar to how a laptop is switched off in emergencies. But in this sense, to the biological robot, this switch-off stopped the heart from beating, effectively killing the robot. The biological robot would die like any human being.

Humans can only hear up to 20kHz, so would not be able to hear this high frequency pitch. A dog whistle is typically within the range of 23 to 54 kHz, and it is said that cats can hear up to 64kHz.

That night, Mich's father went into her bedroom and stood over her. He gazed down at his daughter with tears running down his cheeks. He must have stood for at least 30 minutes, reflecting on the life of his child, for he knew that he was losing the battle, and realised what he had to do. He kissed her gently on the cheek and quietly left the room. During the course of the night Mich's father confided in his peers. Collectively they agreed to reunite Dan and Mich.

66. Tina's Cemetery Visit

During breakfast, Braxton asked Tina if she would like to visit the cemetery during the lunchtime break to see his grandparents' grave. Tina jumped at the chance. She didn't work too far away and loved the thought of sharing some quality time during the day with her partner.

He would pick her up at her workplace and then they would drive to the cemetery together.

They parked in the cemetery's main car park, which was just in front of the entrance's wrought iron gates at the very foot of the hill.

It had been a while now since the police had allowed the cemetery to be re-opened, but they had insisted that the area around the grave should be cordoned off to the public.

"I think I should warn you that it's quite a walk up the hill. Are you ready?" Braxton had a smile on his face as he asked Tina with his arm around her shoulder. She smiled in response.

"It's a beautiful cemetery, Braxton. I like the way the groundsmen have kept the bushes well clipped and the odd arrangement of flower borders including the roses. It's so peaceful here," remarked Tina.

The ground was slightly wet as there had been some rain that morning, and as always the gravel crunched underfoot as they ascended the slope. It was a winding pathway for a very good reason, because this allowed a gentler incline, making the journey to the top of the hill slightly easier... if not slightly longer. Tina also noticed there were several wooden benches evenly placed for people to sit down and rest. Some of them had inscriptions from families who had donated them to the grounds in memory of their loved ones.

"Let's sit for a second. I need to get my bearings. It's a bit of a labyrinth and the last time I came here I found the grave having approached it from the top. Give me a sec..." Tina smiled and wondered if this was just an excuse for Braxton, who sounded a little out of breath. She had noticed he had put on a bit of weight recently.

Braxton wiped the damp bench with a cloth and the pair sat down as he surveyed the mass of graves ahead, trying to figure out where his grandparents were in this maze.

"So where's the other grave, Braxton? The one that had those two weird bodies in them?" enquired Tina.

"They're round the back at the very top, quite a way from here. Why?" said Braxton.

"Oh, no reason, I'm just curious as always. We still have plenty of time, so if you wanted to see it again, I'd be interested to see it too... if I'm allowed?" Tina tried to sound encouraging.

"Well, I guess it's OK. It's just a hole in the ground at the moment. As holes go, it's pretty much standard." They stood up to continue their journey to his grandparents' resting place.

They found it within a couple of minutes.

They stood side by side, holding hands and looking down on a simple grave with a small urn that Braxton had filled with flowers the other day. It was cute. They both kept silent for a moment. Braxton had a smile on his face and seemed content.

"I miss them, even after so many years now. I hope they are together somewhere. Maybe there is a heaven, we'll never know, I guess," Braxton philosophised with Tina.

"Yes. I am sure they are! They are together in peace," Tina felt humble and squeezed Braxton's hand.

"Where are your grandparents? We've never talked about yours," Braxton realised how self-centred he had been.

"Oh don't worry, Braxton. I know you've a lot on your plate at the moment. All my grandparents are long gone. I didn't really know them. I'm quite envious that you had time with yours. It must have been very special," said Tina.

"Where are they?" asked Braxton.

"Oh, they're up north, close to where my parents live. Mum and Dad pop into the cemetery to pay their respects now and again. I think I went there when I was younger, but I don't remember the last time I went."

There was a time of reflection, as they both drifted into their thoughts.

"Come on! Let's go and see that incredible hole at the top!" Tina tried to lighten the mood. She squeezed Braxton's hand as he put his arm around her shoulder and marched up the hill, crunching the gravel on their way in a fun military style.

As they approached the top, Mike popped out of the office and called over as if to say hello. He joined them and they shook hands.

"Hello, Mike, this is Tina, my other half. We've taken a lunch break so I could introduce her to my grandparents'. She was also keen to see the other grave. As I explained, it's just a hole in the ground!" expressed Braxton.

Mike laughed. "Yes! If you've seen one hole, you've seen them all! I've lost count of how many holes I've seen or dug in my lifetime. If I had a penny for every one of them, I'd be a rich man.

"Well, feel free to wander around," he continued. "If you need me, I'll be in the office doing some paperwork. We may dig the graves and keep the grounds, but bureaucracy is bureaucracy in every walk of life." Mike returned to his office and left Braxton and Tina to wander around the area.

"Mike told me that the graves here aren't the oldest in the cemetery, but still date as far back as 200 years ago… should be interesting," said Braxton.

"Yes, there's one here, a huge gravestone, has at least six names on it dating from 1804 through to 1918. Must have been a family called Elton, some lovely names here too. Here's one called Edith, another called Emily, another Elsie. Aren't these old names so adorable? The family must have had a thing for girls' names with the letter E." Tina had started to enjoy herself.

Braxton also joined in. "Wow, look at this one! It's enormous! It goes back three generations from 1786 through to 1890. The gravestone is almost about to topple over and could do with a bit of a clean, but such character! Family name, Wheatcroft, the eldest being Grenville born in 1786, died 1832, so only 46 years old. Times must have been hard way back then."

Braxton noticed Tina approaching the cocoon's open grave. "Hey, don't go too close! Keep outside the cordoned area, Tina. We don't want you falling in, do we!" Braxton was joking, but at the same time he was conscious that he didn't want an accident on his hands, and certainly didn't want to have to report back to Dawson that the grave had been compromised.

Tina had in fact stopped at an adjacent and modestly small gravestone and shouted over to Braxton. "Did you say the two bodies were really tall, Braxton?"

"Yes, why?" he yelled back.

"I think you'd better come and take a look at this!" Tina didn't move her head. She focused on the grave, as if to mark the spot.

Braxton marched over to Tina and put his arm around her side and looked at the gravestone in front of them. As they stood side by side, both of them remained motionless, staring in complete silence as they realised what they were witnessing.

67. Mother and Child

Directly in front of Braxton and Tina lay a fresh bouquet of roses in a multitude of colours. The bouquet must have only been laid there recently at the base of a very old, modest and well-kept gravestone, on which was written:

Elizabeth Daniels 1872 - 1896

Here lies the gentle giant lady

Died of a broken heart

Loving wife to Harold Daniels

Doting mother to Samuel Daniels

Missing at age 3 months

68. Case Closing

DC Braxton had finally drawn his own conclusions about the two bodies found in a cocoon located in an unplanned grave. It was now time to file his report. He started the procedure by going through everything with his superior, DS Dawson. Thereafter, the two would send it to Detective Inspector Baines for completion.

Braxton made a few final amends to his report. He printed it off and handed it to Dawson as they sat together in his office.

Dawson, who had been involved at the start of the case, was quite intrigued about how it had progressed. He knew it was going to be a difficult one to solve.

"So, Braxton, before we go into the detail of your report, what's your conclusion? Let's cut to the chase, so to speak," said Dawson.

"Well, Sarge, I'm afraid there isn't one officially, because there is absolutely nothing to go on. I've tried really hard to hold on to something, something tangible. But, Sarge, you were there! You know there was nothing to go on, other than those crazy results from the autopsy. I'm afraid all we can do is place them in the unsolved file as lost and found, almost the opposite of a missing persons' case. So if someone does report a missing person perhaps we can assess these two then.

"There is no evidence of a murder, nor manslaughter. The man died naturally of a cardiac, and even now George and her team still cannot find a reason for the death of the woman. The only thing George could come up with was that her heart just stopped beating, as if it were a natural death. Yet she was so young looking… so sad.

"Sorry, Sarge! I know it's not what you wanted to hear, but that's it," concluded Braxton, slightly embarrassed and blushing.

"Don't worry, Braxton. To be honest I'm not surprised. But I am curious. Why are you are saying 'officially'? Are you saying you have a theory?" queried Dawson.

"Well, Sarge, the evidence, if I can call it that, suggests something that is very unethical and unnatural, maybe crazy," said Braxton, leaving Dawson slightly puzzled.

"OK, now you have my full attention. I will keep this between us, so don't worry. It won't go beyond these four walls. What is it?" asked Dawson.

"You heard George, Sarge. They had their ages as 120 to 150, and yet they looked in their mid-30s.

"I also projected average heights of countries from the past to the future and the average reaches around 7ft in about 150 years from now.

"The cocoon was made of a material not available, and is only a concept as of today. Perhaps it's a material available 150 years from now.

"Why that cemetery, Sarge?

"Buried next to the two dead bodies' grave we discovered another grave. It was the grave of a woman, a giant of a woman, who had lost her baby. The baby had gone missing, and this was in the late 19th Century! You hear of baby abductions. What if.… what if this baby was taken for a reason, and then returned to its mother after the child had eventually reached a certain age and died?" Braxton stopped in order to draw some breath, and at the same time he noticed Dawson had raised his eyebrows, perhaps in total disbelief.

"I think we should conclude the case, Sarge, and re-bury the two dead bodies in their grave. I think they were returned to be next to their mother." Braxton was relieved to get it off his chest, as he looked at Dawson, waiting to be told he was off his rocker.

"Well. We often have cases that defy explanation. As you say, Braxton, we can't go to the DI with that. But, I do agree it's an unsolved case.

"Also I don't think it's wrong necessarily to propose we return the bodies to the grave as a conclusion. So I will back you up on your official line.

"As for your theory. If I understand what you are saying, then I can't go along with that, other than it makes for a great story. Perhaps something may crop up in the future. So for now, let's close it. Thanks, Braxton. Let's submit the report and move on." Although perhaps secretly agreeing with Braxton, Dawson did not wish to show it.

"OK. Shall I arrange for a re-burial, Sarge?" asked Braxton.

"Yes, start the ball rolling and when we get the OK, make it happen."

"Thanks, Sarge, and thanks for your understanding," said Braxton.

Braxton left the office for some air. He needed some time to reflect on what he had just reported to Dawson, "He must think I'm crazy!" he thought.

That evening Braxton sat with Tina and Joe to explain the conclusion he had reached with Dawson, and his slightly unusual alternative theory.

Joe agreed with Braxton's theory. Even Tina seemed to think it kind of made sense, even though it did sound complete madness.

All three agreed to attend the re-burial of the dead couple. If Braxton's alternative theory was right, then maybe the man's name was Samuel Daniels after all. However, for now the woman's name would remain a mystery. Perhaps she was his sister or wife, as they were of a similar age.

Braxton arranged for one large coffin to be made in order to accommodate the couple. He also gave explicit instructions to the undertakers that the corpses should be buried holding hands again. The coffin would be laid to rest in the same grave in which the bodies were found. He also contacted Mike at the cemetery so that the grave could be prepared for the burial.

69. Laid To Rest

It was the day of the funeral. Braxton had agreed the night before to pick up Tina and Joe en route to the cemetery from his office. Dawson was unable to attend due to other work related engagements, but for Braxton this funeral was covered on his work schedule.

Braxton made all the arrangements. He had ordered two wreaths – one for each of the deceased. To a certain extent he had become a little attached to the dead couple, as had Tina and Joe.

The hearse drove up the cemetery drive and parked adjacent to the open grave. The driver and assistant exited the car, and along with Braxton and Joe's help, the coffin was laid at the side of the grave.

A local priest attended and said a few words as the bodies were laid to rest. He spoke about how they would be together in their next life. The coffin was lowered into the ground and there followed a moment of silence to reflect. The few who attended all had their heads down as they said the Lord's Prayer. Braxton again wondered what this couple had gone through, for indeed they would have each lived a life, just like everybody else. He surveyed the group of people at the funeral, and thought how sad it was to see that the only attendees were total strangers. Although he knew that was to be expected.

Braxton thanked the priest and undertakers as they left. Mike was close by, waiting for the remaining mourners to leave so he could fill in the grave.

Braxton suddenly noticed an old man by some trees in the distance. He had been observing the ceremony, but by the time Braxton finished thanking everyone, he had disappeared.

"Mike, did you see an old man over there by the trees?" asked Braxton.

"No. Sorry, Braxton. But to be honest, I was planning for the burial and preparing. Was there an old man? We often have people like that here. People who pass their time when funerals are under way. Maybe he was one of them. They're typically lonely people who like to watch and observe. You know the type," said Mike.

"Well, he seemed very interested in our proceedings. He seemed quite tall and familiar too. Yes, as you say, perhaps it's just your usual observers, voyeurs...." concluded Braxton, although the thought of who the man may have been didn't leave him for a while.

Braxton went up to Tina and Joe and asked the same question. "Did you see him, the old guy by the trees? He was tall, dressed all in black. Quite a white complexion... Did you see him? I get the feeling I've seen him somewhere before," again repeating the same question.

"Sorry, Braxton, didn't see him," they said in unison.

"OK, then, it's just me. Maybe I'm being a little paranoid or maybe I just need a drink. Let's go to the bar for lunch."

Braxton and the group left the grounds as Mike and his team completed the task of filling in the grave and tidying the surrounding area.

Later that afternoon a very tall and pale old man dressed in black stood over the couple's grave.

70. Rest In Peace

The tall man stood for almost 15 minutes. He just stared at the grave's fresh soil, showing no emotion on his face, with all his thoughts held inside.

He was an old man with slightly wrinkled and gaunt features, blanched skin, and deep set eyes that were slightly dark and sad. He wore a heavy black coat with a hood that covered his head, so it was impossible to tell what colour hair he had, if any at all.

He closed his eyes and remained there for a further five minutes, perhaps reflecting on the two lives that had passed.

He placed a circular wreath of flowers at the foot of the grave, stood up and whispered: "Rest in peace my children. I will always love you Michelle and Samuel. You will be together always." He stayed for another couple of minutes then walked away from the scene.

Braxton was sauntering up the cemetery hill, returning to revisit the grave area. Something had kept niggling him about the man who had been observing the burial ceremony from a distance.

As he climbed the gravelled pathway, he couldn't help but notice the old man again. Braxton was still quite a distance away and so he began to run along the winding path to approach him, but by the time he turned the corner the old man had disappeared.

Slightly out of breath, Braxton stopped at the foot of the grave to recover. All that was in front of him were some wreaths laid out on the grave.

After a couple of minutes, when his heavy breathing had calmed, he focused on one of the wreaths that had not been there before. Written on it were the words *"Rest in peace Michelle and Samuel, Love, Your Father."*

Braxton froze. All sorts of thoughts were racing through his mind, but what could he do? He stood for almost 15 minutes, staring at the words and realising that this old man may have placed this wreath here, and that there could be more evidence relating to this case. He still felt like he had recognised the man, but his recollection was vague… could he have been the man at Hyde Park?

But then he realised this was a wreath of love, of caring, of someone who had lost their closest ones. What would come out of this other than more crazy theories?

Braxton chose to let the wreath lie where it was placed, and to let the loving couple rest in peace. He bowed his head in respect and walked away from the grave for the very last time.

71. *Life Goes On*

It had been a while since the mysterious case involving the two large bodies had been closed. Braxton had quite forgotten all about it as life went on.

Both Dawson and Braxton had been promoted within CID. Dawson had become DI, whilst Braxton had replaced Dawson as DS. In addition, a new DC named Beth Sutton had joined their team. She was a young woman in her mid-20s who had fitted well into their comradery, bonding especially well with Waites who had been requested to take Sutton under her wing.

Braxton and Tina had seen more and more of Joe as he came to the quiz nights on a regular basis, along with other members of his newly formed team, The Carrot Tops. In the team were twins Emma and Emily and one of Joe's college friends named Glyn who originally came from the north of England. Some said he looked very Nordic, being over 6ft tall and with red hair.

It had been a close call as to whether they would call themselves The Gingers. This name had been thought up by Joe, but the girls in particular preferred The Carrot Tops as it had a more comical feel to it.

As expected, Joe had hooked up with Emma and had been together for quite a while now. It had been just a question of time before it would happen, and they had become inseparable since. It was quite endearing to see as they were always holding hands or cuddling.

They also thought that maybe something was going on between Emily and Glyn, for the signs were there for all to see. Between all four of them they were always having fun with plenty of giggles and they also did quite well at the quiz too.

At each quiz night Tracey was becoming bigger and bigger, and everyone wondered if she might be due to give birth sometime soon. Tonight they hadn't seen either Brenda or Tracey at all.

The LGBTs team members Seb and Chaz were at their regular table, sitting next to two other men. Braxton had guessed the men were substitutes for the evening, and maybe another LGBT couple.

Braxton popped over to say hello. He shook their hands and was told that Tracey was in labour. The baby was due any time now.

"How exciting for Brenda and Tracey, about to have their first baby!" said Tina. "Fingers crossed it all goes well," and they toasted the imminent arrival of the new-born.

As the evening progressed, Seb finally received a call. True enough, Brenda and Tracey had just had a baby boy of 9lbs 7oz, or just over four kilos. Both mother and child were doing well and comfortable. A large cheer resounded around the room. Then came another round of drinks, followed by another toast, this time to the new bouncing baby boy.

72. *Life Changes*

The following week at the quiz night the BLTs and The Carrot Tops were quite surprised to see Brenda. She had come on her own and had sat down with the other LGBTs team members at their usual table. Brenda said she would help her team, but wasn't really participating, for her mind was still in dreamland.

She had left the new-born baby sound asleep at home with Tracey. The pair of them had just been allowed out of hospital after a couple of days and were exhausted.

Both Brenda and Tracey had been going through the usual new baby routines – comforting the crying baby, resting, feeding and nappy changing continuously throughout the day and night. On this particular night Brenda had decided to leave Tracey and the baby at home to rest. This gave her an opportune moment to visit the quiz night and give her friends the good news.

"It's just as unbelievable as you might imagine. Never would I have thought that I could have become a father when I realised in my youth that I was a lesbian. I still sleep at night thinking of those days.

"And now here he is, my baby boy. He's so cute! We are calling him James Simon after both our fathers' first names. We thought it had a traditional feel to it, and I know my father is so proud," said Brenda, who just couldn't stop talking, pumped up with adrenalin and excitement.

"He has the eyes of Tracey, my father's nose and my black hair.

"He is so cute. Here, take a look. Here are some photos we took of him. Isn't he cute?" said Brenda as she passed around a number of photos of the baby, held by Tracey or Brenda and an older man, quite possibly Brenda's father.

Braxton couldn't help but remark to himself that the baby couldn't possibly have had Brenda's hair, or her father's nose, as he had inherited no genes from her. But he soon checked himself and realised it was about the romance of it all. Why shouldn't Brenda think that way? Let her believe that, good for her!

"Adorable!" said both Sally and Tina, congratulating Brenda yet again.

"You must be so proud, Brenda," said Seb as Brenda nodded her head, half in tears of emotion.

"Guys, I have to tell you. I want so much to be James's father that I am going to go through a sex change!" Brenda had tears of happiness rolling down her cheeks.

"It's something that I have been discussing with Tracey for quite a long time now, and she is fully behind me. I feel so comfortable about this. It's what I should be. It's what I am inside. I hope you are happy for us?" asked Brenda, seeking support from her friends.

"But of course, Brenda. If you feel so strongly about it, then you should do it. You are so very brave to do this, and I am sure you will be happy," said Tina in support.

The twins and Tina in particular gave Brenda a big hug as the boys Braxton, Joe and Gerry watched on in silence, possibly in shock, whilst Seb, Chaz and the others gave a clap of celebration.

"Yes. From now on, I would like you all to start calling me Brendan instead of Brenda. It kind of helps me to start thinking of the process, and it will help me immensely with your support. Are you OK with that?" Again Brenda was fishing for her friends' acceptance.

"Of course, Brendan," said Sally. "Whatever you say, we will support you. Three cheers for Brendan! Hip hip!" Three cheers ensued as Brendan bought another round of drinks.

73. Ginger Day

Some time had passed, the months had come and gone. Summer was on its way out with the passing of July and August, yet it was still such a beautiful warm and sunny September day.

Braxton had decided to grow his ginger hair a little longer to show off his colour. He had even grown a beard to emphasise the red.

Joe too had allowed his locks to grow almost to shoulder length and had decided to sport a trendy 1970s moustache.

Just for a short period of time, even Tina got in on the act by dying her hair a dark auburn colour. It felt good to dye her hair, as it made her feel closer to Braxton. At the same time she also knew that it was not such an outlandish colour for her, as red hair ran through her family, including her grandmother and aunt.

Tina, Braxton and Joe were in a circle facing each other, along with Joe's friend Glyn and the redhead sisters Emma and Emily. The twins had let their red hair loose from their pony tails to reveal magnificent, long, wavy locks.

All six hooked their arms together and yelled at the top of their voices: "Three cheers for the redheads, yippee!" And they threw their arms up in the air.

Immediately they all turned 180 degrees with their backs to each other, to face hundreds, maybe thousands of redheads of all ages and sizes, all laughing their heads off in celebration.

They had made it to the festival at Breda in the Netherlands, a city largely comprising of medieval buildings, and surrounded by a canal.

It was the first Saturday of September and they just had to do it, they just had to celebrate their race, a kindred of redheads that were not a dying breed but were here to stay.

They were in the city's main square, Grote Markt, which was filled with redheads for as far as the eye could see. An ocean of red, wave after wave of ginger, oh what a joy to behold!

The six of them grabbed their beers and drank, and wandered amongst their people, integrated into their tribe.

74. Made To Order

Meanwhile, back in the 24th Century, L-C2712-03, or Elsie to her friends, sat in front of her console and knew it was time. She was a 62-year-old woman who had another 20 odd years to go in her successful career as a businesswoman, manufacturing unisex clothing.

But now the time was just right. She had been debating this for a number of months, in fact for nearly a year now, with her friends. She was ready to become a parent. It was quite fashionable to start a family at the age of 60 these days.

The thought of settling down and seeking parentage had been with her for quite some time. With it came excitement, trepidation and responsibility. But above all she wanted to love and care for another soul, before it was too late for her.

These days it was simple. She went straight on to BIOROB, one of many sites on the internet where you could order your new biological robot, called biorobot for short.

This site in particular came with a high reputation, although it was perhaps a little bit more expensive than the others. Luckily, money did not matter to Elsie. This was a very important commitment, and she knew she wanted to rely on quality.

There was the usual filling in of personal details online – date of birth, place of birth, address, proof of income and so forth, as well as a signature of authorisation. But the hardest bit was when it came to the selection panel to choose the profile of the new-born.

The selection initially started by asking what percentage of the customer's own DNA they would like their new-born baby to inherit. This could range from 100 per cent down to 0 per cent.

If one chose 100 per cent, they would be warned that effectively this was a clone.

Choosing approximately 50 per cent would mimic natural conception between a man and a woman.

Choosing 50 per cent meant that 50 per cent would come from your DNA and the remainder would come from one of two options. The first would see 50 per cent randomly generated from a gene pool of healthy DNA. Effectively the randomness would be like a lottery using a pool of genes, although based on further selection criteria that followed in the selection panel.

The second option was to link with another person, just the same as any natural conception. However, in this case the other 50 per cent could even come from the same sex. This meant that for the first time, a woman could have a baby with another woman, or a man with another man. This option of naming another person required the permission from the two individuals involved.

0 per cent was effectively similar to adopting a baby based on certain selection criteria.

The selection panel continued. Where possible, the site would give an explanation of each option, how this information is used and, where possible, what type of medical science was involved.

The next selection was for choosing the sex of the baby. A simple choice between male or female. The sex of an individual is determined by a pair of sex chromosomes (gonosomes):

☐ Male Males typically have two distinct sex chromosomes (XY), and are called the heterogametic sex.

☐ Female Females typically have two of the same kind of sex chromosome (XX), and are called the homogametic sex.

Then it came to sexual orientation.

Normally all females have two X-chromosomes, one of which is inactive or switched off in a random manner. Researchers observed that in some women with homosexual sons there was an extreme skewing of inactivation of these X-chromosomes. The process was no longer random and the same X-chromosome was inactivated in these mothers.

This suggested that a region on the X-chromosome might be implicated in determining sexual orientation. The epigenetics hypothesis suggested that one developed a predisposition to homosexuality by inheriting these epi-marks down the generations.

During this epoch most people chose asexual because the other orientations were not popular and regarded as primitive. So much so, that the website owners had thought of removing this selection option, with asexual as the only selection available. However, for the moment the choice was:

- ☐ Heterosexual
- ☐ Homosexual
- ☐ Bisexual
- ☐ Asexual

Then it came to a series of attributes including:

Colour of eyes? So far, as many as 15 genes were associated with eye colour inheritance. Some of the eye-colour genes include **OCA2, gey** and **HERC2**. So choice was:

- ☐ Brown due to **HERC2** being brown
- ☐ Blue due to **HERC2** being blue and **gey** as blue
- ☐ Green due to **HERC2** being blue and **gey** as green

Colour of hair?

- ☐ Black
- ☐ Brown
- ☐ Red   The **MC1R** recessive variant gene gives people red hair and generally results in skin that is unable to tan.
- ☐ Blonde
- ☐ Bald   Equivalent to alopecia. This is caused by approximately eight genes, the main one is known as **ULBP3**, this gene is normally not present in hair follicles

Height? There may have been as many as 20 genes involved, and height genes may have been on the X chromosome and chromosomes 7, 8, and 20. There was also the possibility to regulate height using the manipulation of the pituitary gland, so effectively growth could be controlled at key stages of development.

Ethnic background?

There then followed what could only be described as an enormous list of regions of the world, and a further drill down into smaller areas in order to select an ethnic origin.

Through the centuries this option became less and less relevant. Sexual relationships crossed over boundaries as the world became smaller, and ethnic origins became less meaningful.

With this option it tried to convey what type of ethnic qualities would be found in each option, including the colour of skin.

On the matter of skin colour, the website included a section that talked about future options. These options allowed the buyer to customise the colour of the skin, including colours such as light purple or green. There was even a comment that eventually there would be a possibility to have patterns. Perhaps a tartan to fit with your clan. Watch this space! Coming soon!

Once Elsie made her selection she went to the online checkout, where she was able to see what was in her basket. Often, it was at this point that additional offers or discounts were made on side items, such as a sale on prams, items of baby clothing, toys and baby equipment. Where there was a chance to make further profit, there was a way.

Having confirmed that she had read the terms and conditions, effectively ticking another box, Elsie confirmed the payment method and authorised accordingly.

Instructions were provided where she would need to attend a medical clinic. At the clinic she would have a blood sample and swab taken from her mouth for DNA. These samples would then have to be authenticated and sent to the address provided through a secure courier.

Finally a message came up that congratulated Elsie on her brand new baby.

Delivery would take place in approximately nine months, give or take a couple of weeks on either side of the expected due date, which was provided in the message.

She was also then presented with a certificate of authentication, as proof of purchase. This could then be saved and printed out if she so wished, and maybe hung in the baby's nursery.

Done.

Elsie sat back and started to think of designing a nursery, and what colours to choose.

Oh and goodness! What name shall she call the baby?

How exciting!

∞

The End

Printed in Poland
by Amazon Fulfillment
Poland Sp. z o.o., Wrocław

53300182R00167